Isabelle could handle Spencer when he was fighting with her...when he was angry with her. But this compassionate side was something that ambushed her defences.

She didn't want to like him. She didn't want to respect him. She wanted to hate him. She *needed* to hate him—otherwise he would unravel her tightly bound emotions.

She tucked her hair back over her left shoulder with a sweep of her hand. 'Please leave. I don't want to talk to you right now.'

'This isn't just about the takeover, is it?'

She rolled her eyes as she turned away. 'As if *that* wasn't enough.'

He came up behind her and planted his hands on the tops of her shoulders. It was a gentle anchoring touch that made her want to lean back against him for the support she secretly, desperately craved.

But what if he had another agenda? What if he was only coming in close to exploit her further? Hadn't he exploited her enough? He would woo her to his side, make her say and do things she might later regret. He might wangle her out of even more shares.

Isabelle knew her tongue was dangerously loosened by the champagne she'd drunk. *Champagne?* How ironic. It was the drink of toasts and celebrations, and yet what had *she* to celebrate? Her beloved hotel was no longer hers. Her life was being taken over by a man she didn't know how to handle. Had never known how to handle. He was too powerful. Too sophisticated. Too *everything*.

The world's most elite hotel is looking for a jewel in its crown and Spencer Chatsfield has found it. But Isabelle Harrington, the girl from his past, refuses to sell!

Now the world's most decadent destinations have become a chessboard in this game of power, passion and pleasure...

Welcome to

The Chatsfield

Synonymous with style, sensation... and scandal!

With the eight Chatsfield siblings happily married and settling down, it's time for a new generation of Chatsfields to shine!

Spencer Chatsfield steps in as CEO, determined to prove his worth. But when he approaches Isabelle Harrington of Harringtons Boutique hotels with the offer of a merger that would benefit them both...he's left with a stinging red palm-shaped mark on his cheek!

And so begins a game of cat and mouse that will shape the future of the Chatsfields and the Harringtons for ever.

But neither knows that there's one stakeholder with the power to decide their fate...and their identity will shock both the Harringtons and the Chatsfields.

Just who will come out on top?

Find out in:

Maisey Yates—**SHEIKH'S DESERT DUTY**
Abby Green—**DELUCCA'S MARRIAGE CONTRACT**
Carol Marinelli—**PRINCESS'S SECRET BABY**
Kate Hewitt—**VIRGIN'S SWEET REBELLION**
Caitlin Crews—**GREEK'S LAST REDEMPTION**
Michelle Conder—**RUSSIAN'S RUTHLESS DEMAND**
Susanna Carr—**TYCOON'S DELICIOUS DEBT**
Melanie Milburne—**BILLIONAIRE'S ULTIMATE ACQUISITION**

8 titles to collect—you won't want to miss out!

BILLIONAIRE'S ULTIMATE ACQUISITION

BY
MELANIE MILBURNE

First published in Great Britain 2015
by Mills & Boon, an imprint of Harlequin (UK) Limited,
Eton House, 18-24 Paradise Road, Richmond, Surrey, TW9 1SR

© 2015 Harlequin Books S.A.

Special thanks and acknowledgement are given to Melanie Milburne
for her contribution to *The Chatsfield* series.

ISBN: 978-0-263-25855-4

Harlequin (UK) Limited's policy is to use papers that are natural,
renewable and recyclable products and made from wood grown in
sustainable forests. The logging and manufacturing processes conform
to the legal environmental regulations of the country of origin.

Printed and bound in Great Britain
by CPI Antony Rowe, Chippenham, Wiltshire

An avid romance reader, **Melanie Milburne** loves writing the books that gave her so much joy as she was busy getting married to her own hero and raising a family. Now a *USA TODAY* bestselling author, she has won several awards—including The Australian Readers' Association most popular category/series romance in 2008 and the prestigious Romance Writers of Australia R*BY award in 2011.

She loves to hear from readers!

www.melaniemilburne.com.au

www.facebook.com/melanie.milburne

Twitter @MelanieMilburn1

Books by Melanie Milburne

Mills & Boon® Modern™ Romance

At No Man's Command
His Final Bargain
Uncovering the Silveri Secret
Surrendering All But Her Heart
His Poor Little Rich Girl

The Playboys of Argentina
The Valquez Bride
The Valquez Seduction

Those Scandalous Caffarellis
Never Say No to a Cafarelli
Never Underestimate a Cafarelli
Never Gamble with a Caffarelli

The Outrageous Sisters
Deserving of His Diamonds?
Enemies at the Altar

**Visit the author profile page at
millsandboon.co.uk for more titles**

To Nas Dean.

I am so grateful we met at RWA in Anaheim.

My life would not be the same without you!

Thank you for all you do to make my writing life
run as smoothly as possible. xxx

CHAPTER ONE

NOWHERE ON ISABELLE'S list of things to do before The Meeting was there any mention of cleaning up a fur ball. She looked at Atticus in dismay. 'You do this to me *now*?'

Atticus purred as he indolently lifted a front paw to groom as if to say, *What is your problem?*

Isabelle blew out a flustered breath. 'Why didn't you do this yesterday when I had time to take you to the vet? Why today, when I've got a hundred people filing into the boardroom—' she glanced at her watch and groaned '—like in about five minutes. Argh!'

She pictured the Chatsfield clan striding in—Gene and his eight adult children...and Gene's nephew Spencer Chatsfield and his two younger brothers. Even *thinking* Spencer's name made her blood boil. As if what he'd done ten years ago hadn't been enough. How could she have fallen for someone so hard and so fast when he'd only been playing a game? That was what made her veins throb and pulse with rage. She had been too stupid to see him for what he was. Too gullible and naive to see he was toying with her because he could, not because he wanted to.

Seven months ago he had come breezing back into

her life with a takeover offer. *A takeover offer!* As if she would ever sell anything to him.

But he was up to his old tricks, somehow in the interim gaining forty-nine per cent of the Harrington shares. But at least they were equals now. She had the other forty-nine so he would have his work cut out trying to get them off her.

To get anything off her, including her clothes— *especially* her clothes.

'I should've brought home the smooth-haired tortoiseshell,' Isabelle said as she gingerly picked up the fur ball in a tissue. 'What was I thinking getting a hair machine like you?'

Atticus blinked his green eyes and then lifted his back leg into a position Isabelle as a wannabe yogi could only envy.

'Or a dog.' She flushed the fur ball in the ensuite toilet. 'One of those cute little yappy purse ones. That's if dogs were allowed at The Harrington.' She quickly checked her reflection in the mirror, grimacing at the way her layered hair hadn't sat quite the way she'd wanted it to. 'Or any pet for that matter. You should think yourself lucky I bent the rules to sneak you in.'

She came back out and looked down at her blue-grey Persian cat again. 'Are you sure you're not going to choke to death while I head downstairs?'

Atticus blinked again and mewed. *'Purrht.'*

Isabelle snatched up her bag and phone. 'I hope to God that wasn't a yes.'

Isabelle saw him as soon as she entered the boardroom. He was sitting to the left of his brothers, Ben and James. Dressed in a sharply tailored designer charcoal-grey suit, with an ice-white shirt and black-and-silver-striped tie, he looked every inch the corporate player. Wheeling and dealing was his forte. He thrived on the challenge of the game, be it in the boardroom or the bedroom...especially in the bedroom. *Damn him.*

His sapphire-blue eyes met hers across the space that divided them, making something punch against her heart like the jab of an elbow. His expression was inscrutable. But he'd always had the amazing ability to cloak what he was thinking behind a mask of marble or an enigmatic smile. Unlike her. Over the years she'd trained herself not to be so transparent. But it took so much energy to contain her emotions. Controlling them was like trying to bail out a wave-swamped dingy with a thimble.

She raised her chin and shifted her gaze to encompass the assembled family and hotel management staff. 'I'm sorry I'm late. I was held up with a...a housekeeping issue.'

Leonard Steinberg, the business manager who was chairing the meeting, gave her a smile. 'All sorted now, I hope?'

'Absolutely.' Isabelle looked at the one vacant chair on the other side of the table from Spencer. 'Who are we waiting for?'

'The mystery shareholder,' Spencer Chatsfield said, clicking his pen on and off as his gaze tethered hers.

Isabelle suppressed a shiver as that cultured baritone with its English accent moved down her spine like a caress. *She had to focus.* This was the moment the Chatsfield family were waiting for, the moment when the final two per cent would be brought back to the table. She knew exactly who was going to walk through that door. Had known for quite some time. Had known and wondered how no one else had put the pieces of the puzzle together before now. The blowout in the press would be monumental. The Chatsfields were good at attracting scandals but this one was going to top the lot.

The door opened and in came Isabelle's stepmother, causing no less of a shock to the assembled family than if a vaporous ghost had appeared.

'Mum?'

'You?'

'How could you?'

'Liliana?'

Isabelle felt sorry for all of them, all except Spencer. How Liliana had kept her identity a secret for so long was part miracle, part luck, especially in the digital age of camera phones and social media tagging. But Isabelle had always found her stepmother to be a secretive, elusive type, hard to get close to, even harder to know.

The Chatsfield siblings had been young children—Cara, the youngest, a tiny baby—when their mother had left after suffering postnatal depression, but Liliana never made contact again. Isabelle found it hard to understand how Liliana could have remained incommunicado with her own flesh and blood but she knew her stepmother to be a complicated personality who kept very much to herself. How did it feel for the Chatsfield family to see their mother sweep in like a reclusive Hollywood celebrity who had suddenly decided to reclaim the limelight?

'I know this must be a terrible shock to you,' Liliana said. 'I know you can't possibly forgive me but I would like to explain. But business first.' She turned to Spencer. 'I'm giving you my two per cent.'

Isabelle shot to her feet so fast her chair rolled back and hit the wall behind. *'What?'*

Liliana turned to look at her. 'On the condition you remain as president of the Harrington chain.'

Isabelle opened and closed her mouth but she couldn't access her voice. She felt the colour drain out of her face like one of those cartoon characters she had watched as a child. All of her extremities fizzed as if her blood pressure was dropping. *This couldn't be happening.* Those shares were meant to be hers. It was her dream. Her life's goal was to own a majority share in The Harrington. She'd been working in the hotel since she was in bobby socks. She was a Harrington, for God's sake. The staff were her substitute family. They relied on her to keep things ticking over like clockwork. How could the hotel be handed to someone else who didn't love and nurture it the way she did?

It was *her* hotel, not Spencer Damn-his-eyes Chatsfield's.

'As majority shareholder Spencer will now be CEO of The Harrington, New York,' Liliana said.

Isabelle ignored the rumble of voices from the Chatsfield siblings and their father, Gene, who looked like he was about to have a conniption. Spencer remained composed and silent. Coolly composed. How he must be enjoying this, she thought as a knot of resentment twisted hard and tight in her belly. How he would be getting off on seeing her hopes dashed. He must have known this would be the outcome of the meeting. Why else would he be sitting there as if butter wouldn't melt in his blistering-hot mouth? Had he done something to win over Liliana? Isabelle knew all too well how skilled he was at getting what he wanted by fair means or foul.

Look how he'd showered her with gifts and romantic attention in the past. She had tried not to succumb but in the end she had fallen and fallen hard. But then, how could she not? Back then she had lacked street smarts while he had graduated from the school of charm with first-class honours.

'I'm not working with him!' she said, flashing him a livid glare.

Liliana gave her a placating look. 'I've given this a great deal of thought. Believe me, Isabelle. I know this is the right thing to do. I think it's what your father would've wanted.'

'My father?' Isabelle choked. 'How can you *say* that? He's the one who gave Jonathan forty-nine per cent to throw away in a stupid poker game. Those shares should've been given to me in the first place.'

Liliana let out an impatient-sounding breath. 'Look, I know this is difficult for you to understand but I think it's the best way forward.'

'Why are you doing this?' Isabelle said. 'Why give the shares to him?' She jerked her head towards Spencer without looking at him. She couldn't bear to look at him and see him sitting there gloating over his prize. *The prize that belonged to her.* 'Why not to me? You know how much this hotel means to me. You know how hard I've worked to—'

'Sort it out between yourselves,' Liliana said. She turned to her family—her bewildered and shell-shocked family. 'I can only imagine what you're thinking. But I need to tell you my side of the story…the reasons I left the way I did.'

Gene got up and stalked out with an embittered

curse, slamming the door so loudly the surface of the water in the glasses on the boardroom table rippled.

Liliana let out a sigh and faced the stunned and hurt and shocked faces of her adult children. 'And there goes reason number one.'

Isabelle watched as each Chatsfield sibling dealt with his or her mother's presence after such a long absence. Anger, disappointment, loss, despair and frustration swirled in a torrid whirlpool that was palpable in the air.

But before she could do or say anything Spencer was at her side with a firm hand placed on her elbow. 'I think it's best if Liliana and her family have some privacy right now,' he said.

'But—'

'We have our own business to discuss.' His look was indomitable, his touch on her elbow electrifying, reminding her of the sensual power he'd once had over her.

Still had over her.

She could feel the latent strength of the cup of his hand. *Pull away. Pull away*, her brain insisted. But her body was following another script entirely, one that was firmly anchored in the past. Her body recognised his touch. Responded to it. Reacted to it with a maelstrom of excitement. His touch stirred deep longings, needs she had stoically ignored or blanked out with work. The physical contact with him, as idle as it was, awakened them, activated them into a frenzy of anticipation.

He led her outside and closed the door on the ruckus that had started inside. 'Gotta love a family get-together.'

Isabelle whipped out of his hold before her senses went haywire. 'Get your hands off me.'

His brows lifted as if he found the notion of her anger mildly amusing. 'That's not what you were saying ten years ago,' he drawled in a husky undertone.

Isabelle curled her fingers into her hands so tightly she felt her nails embed themselves into her palms. Hatred swelled in her chest so rapidly and so thickly it was suffocating. She snatched in a scalding breath, glaring at him so furiously it felt as if her eyeballs were on fire. 'I thought I'd made it clear what I thought of you and your business propositions seven months ago.'

He lifted a hand to the left side of his face, stroking it pointedly. 'Slap me again if you dare, but I should warn you that this time there will be consequences.'

Isabelle felt a frisson pass over her flesh at the gauntlet he'd thrown down. She had never been the sort of person to resort to violence. She hadn't hit or slapped anyone or anything in her entire life. But that meeting seven months ago had made something in her snap. She had flown at him like a virago. She could still hear the loud crack of her palm as it connected with his jaw and the way his head had snapped back. In her mind she could still see the crimson print of her hand starkly outlined on his lightly tanned face. He had shown nothing in his expression other than a steely glint in his eyes that had made something deep and low in her belly tremble. That same glint was in his eyes now, warning her, goading her, challenging her. It was having the same physical effect on her. Making her quiver, that shifting-sand feeling behind her knees and between her thighs. How could he still have this effect on her?

She could *not* allow it. It *must* stop. She had to get control of herself.

She swung away and stalked down the corridor in the direction of her office, tossing dismissively over her shoulder, 'I have work to do.'

He caught up to her in two strides and placed a restraining hand on her forearm. '*We* have work to do,' he said, and all but frogmarched her into her office and closed the door with a spine-tingling click as the lock fell into place.

His take-charge manner annoyed the hell out of her and she had a feeling he knew it. What was with all this touching, for God's sake? What did he hope to prove? That she was the same weak little pushover she had been as a naive twenty-two-year-old?

Even though she was wearing silk sleeves she felt his touch sear through her flesh like smouldering coals. She held his glittering gaze as she unpicked his hold, finger by finger, dusting off her sleeve as if it had been contaminated by something disgusting. 'I don't think you heard me, Spencer,' she said through tight lips. 'I want nothing to do with you or your business. If you want to play hotels go find yourself a Monopoly board.'

The corner of his mouth lifted in a crooked arc. 'Ten years on and you're still mad at me?'

Isabelle ground her teeth in an effort to disguise her tumultuous emotions. How dare he ridicule and mock her for still feeling betrayed? How could she *not* feel betrayed? He had deliberately set about seducing her only so he could boast to his friends about 'doing' stuck-up Isabelle Harrington. She could just imagine the ribald laughs they would have shared over a few drinks. Thank God she hadn't told him he'd been her first lover. Deflowering a New York virgin would no doubt have won him some serious bragging rights.

And then there was her other secret, the secret she had told no one but her friend Sophie.

Isabelle slammed the door in her brain where she had locked the pain of the past. She had every right to be infuriated with him and nothing he could do or say would ever change that. He could never undo the damage, even if he still to this day didn't know the full extent of it. 'I have absolutely no feelings where you're concerned,' she said.

Before she could move away he lifted his hand to a stray tendril of her hair and positioned it cosily back behind her ear. His idle touch triggered a frenzy of sensation, all the nerves beneath her skin quaking in reaction. She would have jerked away but she was determined to show him he didn't have the same effect on her he'd had in the past…or at least that was what she rationalised. It was dangerous to allow him this close, dangerous and yet irresistible. He was a powerful magnet and she was a tiny iron filing. She could feel his force field every time she looked at him. It was there in his eyes, the tug of attraction that refused to be subdued. She held her breath as he trailed that same lazy finger along the line of her gritted jaw, back and forth, making her skin tingle with the thrill of his touch. It had been months and months since someone had touched her. Her skin craved the contact. Her whole body trembled and shivered inside the shield of her clothes in its hunger for more.

As if of their own volition her eyes went to his mouth. Something fell off a high shelf in her stomach as she looked at that slanted contour, the vermillion borders defining a mouth that could be hard and yet soft, salty and sensual and devastatingly addictive. She had been kissed since but no one came even close to his mesmerising expertise. No one else had shaken her to the core of her being, evoking a response from hers that was both terrifying and exciting. It was as if his mouth could unlock a part of her personality no one else had ever had access to. He could undo her. Unravel her. Topple her from the very foundations of her being, leaving her in a thousand tiny pieces like a carelessly scattered jigsaw.

His finger glided to the base of her chin and, with the tiniest amount of pressure, raised it so her eyes connected with his. 'That's probably a good thing considering I'm now your boss.'

Isabelle dipped out of his hold and folded her arms across her chest, glaring at him icily. 'I'm not taking orders from you.'

His mouth came up again in that amused arc. 'You heard what your stepmother said. I now have majority share.'

She unlocked her arms and clenched her fists instead. 'How did you get her to give them to you? No doubt by spinning some fantastical tale to woo her to your side. She was *supposed* to give them to me.'

One dark eyebrow lifted. 'Is that a sense of entitlement I can hear?'

Isabelle clenched her jaw so hard it felt like two tectonic plates grinding together. 'I've worked for this hotel since I was a kid,' she said. 'I've spent most of my life learning everything about the business from the ground up. I've worked in housekeeping. I've worked in the kitchen. I've made it my business to understand

every aspect of management. When your aunt captivated my father, *I* was the one who held the fort so the
staff didn't lose their focus. *I* was the one who worked
ridiculously long days to keep things steady. *I* was the
one who came up with the creative plan for the future.
I'm the one who has put everything else in my life on
hold so I can keep the Harrington brand alive and competitive in a constantly changing and challenging market. Liliana of all people *knew* that. She had no right
to hand it to you.'

'They were her shares,' he said. 'She could do what
she liked.'

Isabelle let out a rude word. 'Yes, that just about
sums Liliana up, doesn't it? She does what she damn
well wants and expects everyone else to suck it up.'

His gaze studied her for a lengthy moment. 'How
long have you known?'

'About her being *the* Liliana?'

He gave a single nod, his expression as inscrutable
as ever.

'A while.'

'How long?'

Isabelle pursed her lips. 'I take it you knew before
she walked into that meeting?'

His eyes never wavered from hers. 'I joined a few
dots in the past twenty-four hours. It's hard to hide your
identity these days. A quick search on the internet and
you can find out just about anything about someone,
even if they're doing their best to hide.'

Had he done a Google search on *her*? Isabelle wondered. She could hardly criticise considering she'd been
cyberstalking him for years. Checking on who he was
seeing—not that he saw anyone for long—what places

he visited, where he holidayed. He was known as the Prince of Pickups. Maybe not quite as bad as his cousin Lucca Chatsfield had been before he married, but Spencer could easily install a turnstile in his bedroom.

She blew out a whooshing breath. 'I confronted her about it a few months ago. I felt it was cruel to keep her family in the dark for so long. I understand someone wanting to be a recluse for a bit but what sort of person walks away from a six-week-old baby?'

'Apparently she had postnatal depression.'

Isabelle gave him a cynical look. 'For twenty-odd years?'

He shrugged as if it didn't much concern him. 'She must have known she couldn't keep her identity a secret too much longer.'

A feather of suspicion lifted the hairs on the back of Isabelle's neck. 'Did you bribe her?'

He gave a deep rumble of self-deprecating laughter. 'My, oh, my, you do have an appalling opinion of me, don't you, darling?'

She ground her jaw again. 'Don't call me that.'

He leaned his hips back against her desk and casually crossed one ankle over the other as if he owned the place. But then he did, *almost*. 'What was she like as a stepmother?'

Isabelle let out another tight breath. 'She held us at arm's length, as if she was frightened of what being a stepmother entailed. My father and her were a closed unit. Once she came into his life he had no time for us anymore—not that he had much time for us in the first place. Even work took a back seat, which is saying something, as he'd always put the hotel before everything. He worshipped her. She could get him to do anything for her. That's probably why he never let on to anyone about who she was. It was their little secret.'

'Until you put two and two together.'

She frowned at him in irritation. 'I'm surprised it hasn't come out before now. One photo would have outed her. But then she hated having her photo taken. She'd always pull back and say her hair or makeup wasn't right.' Her arms tightened across her body as if that would somehow contain her bitter disappointment at how her stepmother had betrayed her. 'Of course it all makes sense now.'

'Given your strained relationship with her, why did you think she might give you her two per cent?'

Isabelle wished she hadn't told him all she had. It had come spilling out, revealing far too much of herself. How much she had sacrificed, how much she dreamed and hoped. He would use it to his advantage. Maybe he already had. Although she had never mentioned her stepmother by name during their brief fling ten years ago, he must have sensed her relationship with Liliana was strained. For years Isabelle had tried to connect with her father's new wife but Liliana wasn't the nurturing or confidante type. She kept very much to herself, serving her own interests without showing any interest in that of others, especially three grief-stricken young girls. 'I foolishly thought she'd noticed how hard I worked for the hotel. Seems I was wrong.'

'She gave you a compliment by insisting you stay on as president.'

Isabelle eyed him narrowly. 'Was that her suggestion or yours?'

His expression gave nothing away. 'You think I want you working under me?'

She clenched her fists again. '*Beside*, not under.'

A teasing glint sparked in his blue eyes. 'We could make this grand old hotel rock. Give it a little facelift. Modernise it. Loosen it up a bit. What do you think?'

Isabelle stalked behind her desk, using it as a barrier. Damn him and his double entendres. He swivelled from where he was perched on the corner so he was facing her, his long legs cutting off her only exit. She would have to step over those lean but strong limbs if she didn't want to scramble over the four-foot-high polished walnut filing cabinet on the other side. 'You understand nothing of the class of The Harrington,' she said. 'You Chatsfields are all the same. You think all a hotel has to offer is a comfortable bed with a bunch of feather pillows and fluffy towels and an unlimited supply of alcohol.'

Something moved at the back of his gaze, a camera-shutter-quick movement she would have missed if she hadn't had her gaze firmly locked on his. 'What do you offer here that I can't get at home?' he asked.

She gave him a guarded look. 'You mean in the hotel?'

The twinkle in his eyes reappeared. 'What else could I mean?'

Isabelle flattened her mouth and crossed her arms over her body again. 'I'm sure you've read The Harrington mission statement. We offer luxurious boutique accommodation to an elite and more *dignified* global clientele.'

The corner of his mouth lifted ever so slightly at her emphasis on the word *dignified*. 'So, no riff-raff.'

Her chin went up. 'Absolutely not.'

His eyes kept hers prisoner. Watching, noting, measuring. 'Your profits were down last quarter.'

Isabelle's spine went rigid. 'It was a colder than normal winter. Business always drops off a little in the low season. It'll pick up now it's spring.'

He released her gaze as he picked up her crystal paperweight and turned it over in his hands. She watched those long clever fingers as they moved over the smooth glass. It reminded her of how he had cradled her breasts in his hands. Even the way he was stroking his thumb over the top of the globe made her breasts tingle in memory. She could feel a blush rising on her cheeks as the traitorous heat in her lower body spread. How could he have such sensual power over her after all this time? Her body had never forgotten the pleasure he had evoked. The memory of it still thrummed in her blood. His electrifying touch, the caress of his lips and tongue, the way he moved within her, the way their bodies had been so in tune—it was like a symphony written exclusively for them.

But nothing about Spencer Chatsfield was exclusive. He'd had numerous lovers before her and numerous ones after. He enjoyed the chase. He wasn't interested in building a bond with a lover, taking it to the next level of commitment. He was always on the go for a new challenge, a new focus. That's why he had pushed and pushed to gain The Harrington. It was a prize, a trophy he wanted. Like she had been.

He put the paperweight down and met her gaze. 'How about you show me your best assets?'

She gave him a cutting look. 'I know what you're doing.'

His expression was guileless. 'What am I doing?'

Isabelle compressed her lips until they hurt. 'It won't work. I'm not that silly little fool you deliberately set out to seduce ten years ago.'

His eyes went to her mouth, and then back to her eyes, something softening in the hard planes of his face as if he was remembering what they had shared. 'I never thought you were a fool.'

She tried not to notice how deep and gravelly his voice had become. How his eyes had darkened to a deep inky blue, how his mouth looked so firm and yet so sensually contoured her own lips ached to feel their pressure against them. The primal need he aroused in her was frightening. Why couldn't she control her response to him? Just being in his presence stirred her senses into mania. She became aware of every area of her flesh he had touched in the past, as if being in his presence activated sensors like a tracking device. She could smell the lime notes of his aftershave with its understory of something woodsy and clean and cool and fresh with the sharp tang of outdoors. He'd shaved that morning, but even so she could see the tiny pinpricks of stubble along his jaw and surrounding his mouth. She'd felt that sexy rasp against her skin, the way it had teased her flesh, catching on her softness, reminding her of all that was different between them.

Isabelle gave herself a mental shake-slap-shake. She had to stop thinking about the past and concentrate on here and now. He didn't want her. He wanted her hotel. He was playing with her, luring her in with that deadly Chatsfield charm. She knew exactly what he was thinking. How much more malleable and cooperative would she be if she was in his bed? He would seduce her senseless to get her to sign anything, to agree to anything, in that dazed state of slavish infatuation she had demonstrated in the past. Before she knew it he would have reinvented her hotel into some lurid facsimile of a Chatsfield hotel. The Chatsfields were synonymous with style, spectacle and scandal. The Harrington's reputation as an elegant and luxurious haven would be desecrated.

She straightened her shoulders. 'I'll get the duty manager to show you around the hotel.'

'I want you.'

Isabelle upped her chin. How did he manage to make three words sound so blatantly sexual? 'I have a prior engagement.'

Searing heat passed from his gaze to hers. 'Cancel it.'

She gave him an arctic glare. 'What are you going to do if I don't? Fire me?'

The edge of his mouth lifted as if he was amused at having that sort of power over her. Isabelle didn't find it amusing. She found it nauseating. 'I'm not sure you'd believe me if I told you what I want to do with you,' he said with an enigmatic smile.

Her face flooded with heat. It was the one thing she prided herself on—maintaining her cool composure—and yet with a single look he could melt her resolve like a blowtorch on butter. Getting away from him before she betrayed herself was top priority. 'Don't you realise there are laws regarding sexual harassment in the workplace?' she said.

His eyes studied hers for a pulsing moment. 'Are you dating anyone?'

'Yes.' The lie was easy. Providing evidence would be the kicker. Isabelle did a quick run-through of her contacts. Surely there was someone she could call on to pose as a stand-in date. If not, she would try Internet dating. One way or the other she would find someone. How hard could it be?

If he was disappointed in her answer he certainly didn't show it. 'When will you be back from your appointment?'

'Why?'

'I'd like to run through some ideas with you.'

Her eyes narrowed. 'What sort of ideas?'

He gave a soft laugh. 'Anyone would think I had a bulldozer waiting at the front door to plough down the place as soon as your back was turned.'

She gave him a hardened look. 'It wouldn't surprise me. There isn't a lot of subtlety about your methods.'

His crooked smile made something inside her chest tighten so she couldn't inflate her lungs. 'I'll meet you in my office at five p.m. There are other things I have to see to first.'

'Fine.' Isabelle gave his legs a pointed look. 'Do you mind?'

He pulled them back towards the desk and waved a hand for her to pass. 'After you.'

She eyeballed him. 'I'm not leaving you alone in my office.'

'What?' The twinkling look was back in his eyes. 'Do you think I'm going to go through your drawers?'

Isabelle blushed so hotly she could feel it prickling over her scalp. She sucked in a breath and made to go past him but he stood just as she did. He towered over her, his body so close to hers she could feel the warmth of it radiating towards her like the glow of a sun lamp.

He grazed the back of her tightly clenched hand with

a lazy fingertip. 'Isn't it time we quit with the pistols-at-dawn routine? We're batting for the same team now.'

Isabelle pulled her hand back close to her body and glared at him, her lips so tight she could barely spit the words out. 'I despise everything about you. This is nothing but a game to you. You've deliberately set out to gain the advantage, working in the background using whatever means you could to outwit me. But I'm not giving up without a fight. You might control the majority share but you can't control me.'

His eyes blazed back, the first sign she had nettled his cool control. 'That's rich coming from you. Who was the one who tried to undermine me by using their friend to get the scoop on my brother James? But that spectacularly backfired, didn't it?'

Isabelle gave a cough of scornful laughter. 'And what about *you*? Getting your brother Ben to *pretend* to be engaged to my sister to drum up a press fest? But that didn't work out quite the way you planned, did it? He and Olivia fell in love for real.'

'More fool them.'

'Oh, yes, that's exactly what you would say, isn't it? You're the "use them and lose them" type.'

'Damn it, Isabelle,' he said. 'I did not use you.'

She drew herself up to her full height, giving him a fulminating glare. 'How much did you win?'

His savage frown made him appear older than his thirty-four years. 'Look, it was a silly joke between a couple of mates. It was crass and I'm sorry you found out about it.'

Isabelle's eyes flared in outrage. 'You're *sorry* I found out about it? How about being sorry for actually doing it, damn it!'

He scraped a hand through his dark brown hair as he let out a muttered curse. 'All right,' he said heavily. 'I'm sorry.'

Isabelle refused to be mollified with an apology that was ten years too late. As far as she was concerned he could never atone for what he'd done—for how he'd made her feel. For the emotional trauma she went through. Putting the pregnancy aside—*because she did not think about that anymore*—she had lost the little confidence she'd had. It had taken her years to date again and even now she avoided the whole process of trying to establish trust with someone she didn't know. She could never relax, to be herself. She was always on guard in case someone took advantage of her. These days she used men like Spencer had used her. Sex was sex. It was a physical need she satisfied just as she would thirst or hunger—when she felt like it. Not that she put herself out there much. She could barely recall the last time she'd had sex except to remember it wasn't particularly satisfying.

'You can keep your apology,' she said. 'As far as I'm concerned we can never be anything but enemies. There isn't a person on this earth I hate more.'

'You know what they say about keeping your enemies close.'

Isabelle gave him a withering look. 'Dream on, Chatsfield. I'm already taken.'

CHAPTER TWO

SPENCER PRESSED HIS lips together as the door slammed in his face. *That went well*, he thought. He let out a long sigh and turned around and surveyed the neat organised office Isabelle had just stormed out of in spite of insisting she wouldn't leave him in it alone. The polished antique furniture and the classic soft furnishings were a visible statement of Old Money. A little old-fashioned for his taste but he could see the appeal for the high-end market.

Isabelle thought he was playing at hotels, did she? She hadn't pulled in a decent profit since her father died the year before. He didn't want to rub her nose in it but if she didn't ease off with the insults he would have to take his gloves off. He wasn't going to have his name associated with anything that wasn't successful. He had a point to prove to his family and he was not going to let little axe-grinding Isabelle Harrington stand in his way.

It had been fun outmanoeuvring her over the past few months. He liked the challenge of outsmarting her. She gave as good as she got, which secretly impressed him. He hadn't noticed that streak of stubbornness in her ten years ago.

Ten years.

How could it have been that long? She was even more beautiful at thirty-two. Her black hair was as glossy as a raven's wing; her brown eyes were the colour of a single-malt whisky, her skin as clear and pure as porcelain. She had a slender figure, not rail thin but curves where a man wanted curves to be.

How could he have forgotten how gorgeous she was? When he'd seen her seven months ago he'd felt the same knockout punch to his guts. The way she walked into the boardroom earlier snatched his breath clean away. Not that he'd shown it, of course. If she knew half of what he was thinking he'd be toast. Her hair had been swinging around her head and shoulders in layered waves, her lush mouth primed in a confident smile. Had she just come from her lover's bed? He hadn't heard a whisper about her love life. He'd got the impression she lived and breathed work. The thought of her with someone else was like a sudden toothache—annoying, distracting, painful. He wasn't the jealous type...or at least he hadn't been until now. He'd never had a reason to be. He didn't hold any woman long enough for the right to feel a sense of loyalty from her.

But for the past few months something about Isabelle had gnawed away at him, a nibble at a time. He liked that she was prepared to stand up to him. She tried to countermove him at every point. She was smart, she was disciplined and she was tactical. She wasn't intimidated by the Chatsfield name, although she had no idea he had no real claim on it. No one, apart from his brother Ben, knew Michael Chatsfield wasn't Spencer's real father.

The empty feeling he got whenever he allowed that

thought to drift into his mind was like having his guts scraped out with a rusty spoon. The loss of his identity, ripped away from him when he'd overheard a few angrily thrown words between his parents as an adult. *His parents.* What a sick joke. His mother had always acted towards him as if he were an embarrassment to her. She could barely bring herself to touch him. He couldn't remember the last time he'd been shown any affection or warmth. It took until that wretched Christmas when he was twenty-nine to figure out why. It didn't matter how hard he worked to please her or his father. He could ace straight A's in school and bring home every sporting trophy he could get his hands on. Nothing made either of them proud and accepting of him. Nothing he did ever made him feel loved or wanted.

It annoyed him that he still struggled with it. He felt he should have put it behind him by now. He was moving on with his life. He had goals and plans. He didn't need his mother or Michael.

He didn't need anyone.

Spencer went to the window overlooking Central Park, which was abloom with cherry blossom and the bright lime green of new growth on the trees and grasslands. New York in any season was vibrant and exciting, but in spring it had a magical energy about it, a sense of hope and positivity and expectancy.

He had to make The Harrington his in every sense of the word. It was his trophy to claim, to show his family he had a right to the Chatsfield name, even if Chatsfield blood didn't flow in his veins. So what if he was a little ruthless? Wasn't every successful person?

He couldn't allow sentimentality to get in the way of a good business deal.

Although there was a small corner of his mind that allowed Isabelle had been badly done by. Her older brother, Jonathan, was a waste of space and had proved that notion by allowing Spencer to think Isabelle was agreeable to his takeover bid. Spencer had already assured Gene Chatsfield the deal was in the bag, so when Isabelle had roundly slapped him down he'd had to regroup, to come up with a different plan to convince his uncle he hadn't done the wrong thing in promoting him as CEO.

Spencer knew he would have to tell Isabelle about her brother's treachery at some point, but he knew from experience how difficult familial relationships were. It had taken years for him to reunite with his brother Ben after he'd found out the truth about his biological origins.

He knew he could also tell her that he wasn't the one who had orchestrated that stupid bet. His mate Tom from university had heard about the beautiful American girl he'd met at a party in London while she was studying at business college. Unbeknownst to Spencer, Tom had laid money with another mate on how long it would take Spencer to get her in bed. Isabelle had found out about the bet via a mutual acquaintance who—like her—assumed he was the one behind it. He had taken offence at her ready assumption he was responsible for something so puerile and offensive. But at the time he'd been too proud and stubborn to defend himself. It wasn't in his nature to beg or grovel. If she believed him capable of such nonsense, then what did it matter? It hadn't occurred to him to fight for the relationship—or at least not then. With him based in London and her based in New York their relationship would have fizzled out sooner or later anyway.

But over time, the fact *she* had ended their relationship and not him had begun to annoy him. To agitate him like a blister that wouldn't quite heal. He'd considered contacting her and explaining the circumstances surrounding the bet, but then Tom had been killed a few weeks later in a skiing accident and Spencer had decided to let his mate's reputation rest in peace.

It left a sour feeling knowing that Isabelle hated him so vehemently now. It seemed so petty. Lots of exes managed to get over their differences over time, and some even became friends. The takeover didn't help matters but at the end of the day she was a businesswoman at heart. Surely she could see this was the only way forward?

But then, he wasn't here to win a popularity contest. He was here to win. Period. He had to make this deal work, otherwise it would prove every lingering doubt he'd harboured since finding out he wasn't the firstborn son of Michael Chatsfield.

He was a bastard, a product of an illicit affair his mother had had as a payback to Michael for neglecting her. He hadn't even had the chance to meet his real father, as he had died some years before. It left a blank hole inside him, a gaping hollow space that could never be filled. The knowledge of his illegitimacy set him apart from the Chatsfield family like a mongrel dog stands out at a pedigree show. No matter how hard he worked, no matter how committed he was to the Chatsfield brand—he would never belong.

* * *

Isabelle went back to her suite to check on Atticus. He was stretched out on the middle of her bed and opened one eye as she came in before closing it again. 'Nice to be some people,' she said. 'I wish I could spend all day in bed.' Her belly gave a little quiver as she thought of Spencer and how his touch had short-circuited her senses. She clenched her jaw. '*Alone.* Just in case you're thinking I still have a thing for him, which I don't. Chatsfield men are all the same. He's arrogant and up himself. He thinks he can pick up where he left off. I saw it in his eyes. I know what he's thinking. He's looking for someone to pass the time with while he's here. But I'm not falling for that. Oh, no.'

Isabelle scrolled through her contacts on her phone to call the vet, but was quickly reassured that unless Atticus was coughing or vomiting excessively he would probably be fine as long as she groomed him regularly and gave him a bit of butter in his food to aid his digestion. She put down her phone and looked at the purring cat. She sighed and leaned over and stroked his silky thick fur. 'I didn't really mean it about the tortoiseshell.'

She glanced at her laptop where she'd left it next to her bed. She'd always thought Internet dating was a little desperate, but heck, she *was* desperate. She had to get herself a date or two before Spencer got under her skin, inside her head or—worse—inside her heart.

She logged in on a popular site and within a few minutes had organised a drink after work with an IT guy called Jacques from Cobble Hill. How easy was dating these days? Just wait till she told her sister Eleanore, who was always banging on about her having no work/life balance.

Isabelle went back downstairs but on her way to her office Enrico Perez, the duty manager, intercepted her. 'Miss Harrington, we're putting Mr Chatsfield in the Manhattan-side penthouse suite on your floor.'

Her heart gave a pony kick against her breastbone. 'He's staying in-house?'

'I hope that's not a problem?' Enrico said. 'He's only here for a week or two while he sorts out the takeover.'

She gritted her teeth. Did everyone have to keep reminding her? Takeover schmakeover. She was sick to death of Spencer gloating over his win. The press would be running wild with the news by now. They had been following her cat-and-mouse battle with him for months. She'd been ignoring calls for the past hour from nosy journalists. Every network would be flashing with the headline *Successful Takeover of Harrington by Chatsfield Chain.* It made her want to puke. 'Isn't there any other suite you can give him?' she said. 'What about the Madison or the Roosevelt suite?' *What about another hotel!*

Enrico shook his head. 'Both are booked out for the next three weeks. We could put him in one of the standard suites, but I thought you'd like to show him what The Harrington can offer in terms of top-end luxury.'

Isabelle chewed at the inside of her mouth before blowing out her cheeks. 'Fine. But why the hell doesn't he stay at The Chatsfield? Or if he's so wealthy, why not in his own Upper East Side apartment?'

'Maybe he's like you,' Enrico said evenly. 'He likes to live and breathe work.'

She pressed her lips together, sending him a defensive look. 'I do have a social life, you know.'

'I'm very glad to hear it,' he said. 'You've worked extremely hard for the hotel. But it would be a shame if you didn't have someone to share the burden with.'

She straightened her shoulders. 'I don't consider it a burden.'

Or at least I didn't until this morning when Spencer Chatsfield strode into town.

'Are there any special touches you'd like to put in Mr Chatsfield's suite?' Enrico asked. 'He's with the family in the boardroom so now would be a good time to show him some of the bespoke service The Harrington is famous for.'

Isabelle felt a spurt of devilry galvanise her flagging spirits. 'Leave it with me. I'll make up his room myself.'

The housekeeping staff had just finished cleaning the room when Isabelle arrived with a hotel tradesman carrying two large mirrors on a luggage trolley. 'Thanks, Rosa,' she said. 'I'll sort out the rest for Mr Chatsfield's stay.'

'Yes, Miss Harrington,' Rosa said.

Isabelle directed the tradesman to the bedroom. 'Hang one mirror on the ceiling and the other on the wall at the foot of the bed.'

The tradesman's brows lifted. 'The new CEO specifically asked for these?'

She gave him a cool tight smile. 'You know what those Chatsfield boys are like. Better make sure the ceiling one is secure. We wouldn't want it to fall down and flatten him in the middle of a threesome, now would we?'

Isabelle waited until the tradesman had completed the task and left the suite before she opened the large tote bag she'd brought with her. She smiled a cat's smile as she took out the array of colourfully packaged condoms in every texture and colour she'd bought at a local pharmacy. She propped them packet by packet in a high tower on the bedside table along with a maxi pump pack of lubricant. She put some handmade chocolates on the pillow, which she'd quickly got the chef to pipe Spencer's initials on. There was a bottle of French champagne—the one she knew Spencer preferred—in an ice bucket and two crystal Harrington glasses, each with an engraved *H* in silver. She took out two long black satin ribbons a metre each in length and tied them to the bedposts in giant bows. She hung a pair of handcuffs on the top knob of the bedside drawer and laid a velvet blindfold on one of the pillows. She scattered some fresh rose petals all over the bed and then stepped back to admire her handiwork.

'Very nice,' a deep male voice said from behind her.

Isabelle whirled around so quickly she felt lightheaded. But maybe that was more to do with seeing Spencer standing there with a satirical smile on his face. She quickly schooled her features into her icemaiden mask. 'Just checking your room is tailor-made to suit your requirements.'

His blue eyes shone with a spark of amusement... or was it mockery? She could never quite tell. 'You Harringtons certainly know how to fine-tune the personal touches.'

She kept her gaze trained on his even though she could feel her face glowing with betraying heat. 'If there's anything I've overlooked, then please let me know.'

He glanced at the mirror on the ceiling and then the bed with its lurid accoutrements. 'No whip?' he said, still with that glinting smile.

Isabelle suppressed a traitorous rush of lust as his eyes moved over her body and gave him an arctic look instead. 'I decided against one in case you start cracking it in places it's not welcome.'

He sauntered over to the table and lifted the bottle of champagne out of the ice bucket. 'Will you join me?'

She hitched her chin to a sanctimonious height. 'I never drink on the job.'

'Surely one small one to celebrate the takeover won't hurt you?'

Isabelle ground her teeth until she was sure they were down a centimetre. 'You're lapping this up, aren't you? Any chance you get you want to rub my nose in it. Next you'll be saying we should have a party to celebrate your latest acquisition.'

He gave her an indolent smile. 'How'd you guess?'

Her mouth dropped open. 'You're serious?'

His eyes held hers. 'Never more so, and I want you to organise it.'

Isabelle swung away with a muttered swear word, holding her arms so tightly around her body her lungs could barely inflate enough to breathe. Was there no end to this humiliating torture? Why was he doing this? It would be excruciating to have to celebrate the takeover in public, to put on a happy face as if all was right with her world. The world he had all but *stolen* from her. 'You're un-freaking-believable.'

'You've held functions here before, have you not?'

She turned and speared him with a fulminating glare. 'Yes, but none with topless dancing girls jumping out of cakes.'

The corner of his mouth twitched. 'My cousin Lucca doesn't have those sorts of parties now he's married to Lottie.'

'I'm very glad to hear it.'

He rubbed his chin between his index finger and thumb in a musing fashion, the sound of his stubble catching on his skin making Isabelle's insides coil tightly with desire. She remembered all too well how sexy his raspy skin felt against her smoother one. How it had left red marks on her face when he'd kissed her. *Why, oh, why couldn't she forget?* If only she could wipe her memory of him, of all she had experienced in his arms, then maybe she could get through this with at least some fragment of her pride intact.

'I was thinking something a little more classy,' he said.

She gave him a contemptuous look. 'Somehow that's not a word I readily associate with you.'

The line of his mouth hardened a fraction but then his phone rang and he dismissed her with a look as he answered it. 'I released a press statement this morning,' he said to the person on the phone. 'I already gave an interview half an hour ago. Yes, that's right. Miss Harrington is delighted with the outcome and is as we speak organising a ball to celebrate the takeover.'

Isabelle glared at him, mouthing, *'What the...?'*

He held up his hand like a stop sign. 'Yes, we have an excellent working relationship...Yes, you can quote me.' He clicked off his phone and slipped it back in his trouser pocket. 'Journalists. I swear I've had fifty calls and it's not even lunchtime.'

She flattened her mouth. 'You told them I was *happy* about this? Are you out of your mind? Who's going to believe it?'

'Do you know nothing about marketing?'

Isabelle aligned her shoulders, bristling with impotent rage. 'You have no right to speak to the press on my behalf. I'll give my own exclusive interview when I'm good and ready and tell them what a prize jerk you are.'

A muscled tightened near his mouth and his blue eyes hardened to flint. 'You want people to come to this hotel?' he said. 'Then you have to show them this is a place that's buzzing. Not with gossip and innuendo but with a can-do vibe. Show a little professionalism, Isabelle. You've got a good product but you're not showcasing it to its potential.'

She glared at him all the more furiously, her heart pounding with a surge of adrenalin. 'So you're basically telling me I'm crap at my job? Is that what you're saying?'

He raised his eyes to the ceiling in a God-give-me-patience manner. 'Look, let's sit down and discuss this like two adults and...'

She planted her hands on her hips. 'So now you're implying I'm childish.'

He drew in a deep breath and released it. 'You're giving a very fine impression of a kid having a tantrum because things haven't gone your way. Quit it with the teddy tossing so we can get on with the job of running this hotel.'

Isabelle stepped right up to him, poking a finger to his sternum. 'Take that back. *Now.*'

He stood like a block of marble. Intractable. Immovable. His steely gaze holding hers in an unwavering lock that made the floor of her belly shiver like a breeze whispering across the surface of a lake. 'I'm not apologising for stating a fact,' he said. 'Grow up or get out.'

She drilled her finger further into the concrete-hard wall of his chest. 'You want me to leave? Then you'll have to carry me out because I'm not go—*hey!* What the hell are you doing? Put me down!'

He scooped her up and carried her fireman-style to the door of his suite. Isabelle drummed his back and shoulders with her fists, kicking her legs up and down like a kid having a tantrum—the irony of which didn't escape her—but she was beyond caring. How dare he treat her like this? What if one of her staff saw her carried out of his suite like a sack of potatoes? She would never live it down. Hatred surged like a flood inside her. It threatened to burst out of every pore of her skin. She dug her fingernails into his back, intent on inflicting as much physical hurt as the emotional hurt he was inflicting on her.

He let out a vicious curse and dumped her unceremoniously on the floor in front of him. The only reason she landed on her feet and not on her head was because he had dragged her down the front of his body, every hard plane and contour coming into contact with hers. 'Stop it, you crazy little wildcat,' he growled.

Isabelle was breathing hard. How she would love to wipe that imperious look off his too-handsome face, but his hands had shackled hers. She felt the steel bracelet of his fingers overlapping her wrists where her pulse was skyrocketing. His touch burned her, ignited her senses into a heated frenzy. She knew if she didn't get away from him she would shamefully betray herself.

She tried to bring her knee to his groin but he countered it by pushing her back against the office door, his arms pinning hers either side of her head in a cage of latent male strength. '*Don't* even think about it.'

She gave him a gimlet glare, trying to ignore the warm minty scent of his breath as it mingled with hers. Trying to ignore the unbearable temptation of his grimly set mouth. Desperately trying to ignore the ridge of his swelling erection in response to her being flush against him. Her body recognised the primal call of the flesh, of the urge of raw earthy lust she had suppressed for most of her adult life. He triggered it like no one else could. It was a force that was as unstoppable as a rising king tide. She could feel it moving in her blood, the pulse of need so strong, so consuming, it overcame any mental obstacle she had put up to resist him. Her pelvis ached to get even closer as the heat and potency of his arousal hardened. The air was so thick with erotic tension it all but vibrated. 'You never used to be so caveman-ish,' she said. 'Or have things got so desperate you have to club your partners into submission?'

His eyes dipped to her mouth, his hands around her wrists loosening a fraction. 'I really want to kiss you right now but something tells me that would be dangerous.'

She gave him an arch look. 'Because I'll scratch your eyes out?'

He gave a low chuckle of laughter. 'That's not the only risk.' He tipped up her chin, his thumb pressing down on her lower lip, on and off like he was pressing a switch. 'Kissing can lead to other things.'

'Face slaps?'

His smile was ruefully lopsided. 'I probably deserved it given the circumstances.'

Isabelle frowned. 'What circumstances? You wanted my hotel and you brazenly came after it. What other circumstances can there be other than your bull-headed arrogance?'

He dropped his hold and stepped back from her. 'Your brother gave me the impression you were okay with the takeover.'

Her frown deepened. 'What? And you believed him given our history?'

He rubbed a hand over the top of his head. 'Yeah, I know. Dumb of me, but I didn't know he knew about our history. Hardly anyone did, remember?'

Isabelle remembered all too well, and when their fling had ended she was immensely grateful for it. For some reason Spencer had kept her out of the eye of the press, unusual for him at the time. Also unusual was the fact their relationship hadn't been a one-, two- or three-night stand. It had actually been a relationship... or so she had thought. He had seen her for close to a month, every night, even during the day when his work schedule and her study timetable allowed. That was why her expectations had been so ridiculously high, foolishly naively high. He had never shown any other girl the attention he had shown her. He had made her feel as if she was someone special. He had bought her gorgeous jewellery and bunch after bunch of flowers, expensive chocolates, champagne suppers, taken her dancing till the wee hours in exclusive intimate clubs where the press didn't harass them. She had allowed herself to think he was falling in love with her. She had even thought he was going to propose to her, that he was only biding his time so as not to rush her. How could she have not seen it for what it was? No wonder he'd kept her away from the press. He hadn't wanted his reputation as a playboy tainted by such seemingly smitten behaviour.

All her girlhood dreams of being swept off her feet by a handsome man who saw her as his soul mate were destroyed when she'd heard about the wager. The hurt had been devastating. Crushing. Cutting her hopes to shreds. Leaving her bitter and angry and feeling exploited in a way she had never felt before. She had given him everything of herself and yet she had been little more to him than a game.

But then to add salt to an already festering wound, a couple of weeks after their breakup she'd found out she was pregnant. The shock had been paralysing. She did a total of twenty tests, one after the other, day after day, week after week, desperately hoping it was a mistake, that she'd somehow misread the results. But each and every time the two lines would appear.

Her mind couldn't accept it even as her body started to show the signs—the nausea, the breast tenderness, the relentless tiredness. How could she possibly be pregnant? The question had been on a constant loop in her brain. They had used protection every time. It couldn't possibly be true. She went even further into a state of denial, burying herself deep in it in the desperate hope that things would magically return to normal.

Week after week went past and still she kept the knowledge to herself, unable to think of how to handle a baby and her career, not to mention telling Spencer he was to become a father.

Her confusion over the prospect of becoming a mother and thus being tied to Spencer for ever through the bond of their child had added another layer of anguish. She didn't feel comfortable with the idea of a termination but neither did she want to be in contact with Spencer. Ever.

But just as she was starting to get her head and heart around the idea of being a mother she'd lost the baby just before the four-month mark. She told no one but Sophie. The only thing she had left of her tiny baby was an ultrasound image. It had been a little girl.

'In hindsight I should've realised you wouldn't let the hotel go without a fight,' Spencer said into the bruised silence. 'But he was pretty convincing, said you were on board with it. That you thought it was a good move forward for The Harrington.'

Isabelle rolled her eyes and moved away from the door, pointedly rubbing at her wrists where his hands had imprisoned her. 'Did you think of calling me first to see what I thought about it?'

He looked at her for a long moment. 'Would you have taken my call?'

She let out a long whoosh of a breath. 'You may have a point.'

Another little silence passed.

'I know you're angry about the way things have been handled,' he said. 'I would be too, if the roles were reversed. But I want this to work, Isabelle. I want to make The Harrington a success. But I can't do that if you're working against me. We have to do this as a team or not at all.'

Isabelle pulled at her lower lip with her teeth. 'What if we don't share the same vision for the hotel? You're a Chatsfield. You have that brand hardwired in your DNA.'

'It's not as hardwired as you think.'

She looked at the suddenly grim set to his mouth, the hardened line of his jaw, as if he regretted his statement. 'What do you mean?'

A distant look came into his eyes as if he had cordoned off a section of his personality: No Entry. Even the way he folded his arms across his broad chest warned her about going any further. 'Tell me what your vision for the hotel is. Give it to me in three words.'

Isabelle smoothed her hands down the side of her pencil-slim skirt. 'Private. Exclusive. Luxurious.'

He gave a slow nod. 'How is that different from any of your closest competitors?'

She found it hard to hold his penetrating gaze. Could he see how out of her depth she felt with him grilling her like an underling who hadn't made the grade? 'We at The Harrington offer boutique luxury unrivalled by our competitors.'

'How do you know?' he asked, still nailing her with his gaze. 'Have you stayed at a competitor's recently?'

Isabelle pushed her lips out on a breath. Talking to him always felt like a fencing match. He would always try and catch her off guard. 'Not…recently.'

'When did you last stay in a hotel other than your own?'

She gave him a churlish look. 'Unlike some people who do little else but gallivant about the globe having exotic holidays I have a job that takes up a lot of my time.'

'Part of succeeding in this business—in any business—is knowing what you do better than anyone else and cashing in on it.'

Isabelle lifted her eyelids in a scathing manner. 'I bet you never fail to cash in on your talents.'

The corner of his mouth tilted. 'Even after all this time you know me so well.'

She tightened her mouth. 'What exactly is the point of this conversation?'

'Clear your diary for the weekend after next.'

'What for?'

'We're going on a mission.'

She curled her top lip. *'We?'*

His eyes were locked on hers. 'We'll spend the two nights checking out the competition. Make notes. Comparisons. See what we can work on to lift our game.'

Isabelle looked at him in alarm. 'You're asking me to spend the weekend…with *you*?'

His expression was poker-faced. 'The idea doesn't appeal?'

She glowered at him. 'You have a nerve.'

'We don't have to share a room, although it will keep costs down if we did.'

She gave him a pointed look. 'Aren't you forgetting something? I have a boyfriend. He's not going to take too kindly to me going off for a weekend with my… my…' She snapped her mouth closed and sent him a glacial look.

His eyes danced with amusement. 'You can't say it, can you? The word is boss. B.O.S.S. Say it, Isabelle. It won't kill you.'

Isabelle pinched her lips together and glared at him. She hadn't thought it possible to hate someone so much. Was there no end to this man's ruthlessness? He was after her pride but she would rather die than relinquish it to him. Rage pounded in her bloodstream. She could feel it roaring in her ears. Her hands curled into tightly balled fists and the urge to hit out at him was so frighteningly tempting she could feel every muscle in her body tensing as taut as steel cords. She was physically shaking with the effort of keeping control. No other man could do this to her. It horrified her that he could so easily dismantle the professional and cool civility she prided herself on maintaining. He had the potential to turn her into a wild woman, a wanton lustful tigress who would do anything to ease the primal ache of her loins. The ache he activated with just a look or a touch.

He stepped closer and lifted her rigid chin between his finger and thumb. 'Say it.'

Isabelle held his gaze even as it scorched her to the core of her being. 'You can't *make* me do anything.'

His eyes glinted with dangerous magnetism. 'Are you sure about that?'

'Perfectly.'

His eyes warred with hers for endless seconds before they lowered to her mouth. Isabelle held her breath, her own mouth parting involuntarily as his breath mingled with hers. He brought his mouth to within a millimetre of hers, the dance of his breath teasing the surface of her lips until she ached and throbbed to press them to the firm possession of his. But she knew his holding pattern was a test. A game. He was waiting for her to be the first one to break. To give in to the attraction that had always arced and fizzed like a current between them.

With a will she had no idea she possessed she stepped back from him and gave him a look as cold as a blast of air off the North Pole. 'I hope you find your room comfortable. If there is anything else you require, please let the duty manager know.'

There was no sign of the physical let-down she was feeling on Spencer's face. His was as unreadable as a mask, all but for a tiny gleam in his eyes that suggested he knew just how close she had been to succumbing to the temptation he'd dangled before her. 'So far the service has been impeccable,' he said. 'I anticipate all my needs will be satisfied by the time my stay has ended.'

She pursed her mouth and swung for the door, her movement stiff and jerky as if her limbs had turned to jointed timber like those of a wooden puppet.

'I want a plan on my desk for the ball by five this afternoon,' he said. 'Is that doable?'

Isabelle threw him a flinty look. 'Will that be all?'

He reached over and picked up a packet of condoms and inspected them for a moment. 'These are two small.' He held up a packet as if to toss them to her. 'Maybe your boyfriend would like them?'

Isabelle gave him a blistering look and left without another word...well, apart from two shockingly rude ones.

CHAPTER THREE

SPENCER SMILED AS he looked at the room Isabelle had prepared for him. The feistiness of her character stimulated him. Made him want to push her buttons to see how long it would take for her to give in to the need he saw every time their gazes locked. He hadn't considered having a fling with anyone while he was here but the notion was more and more appealing, especially with her giving off her haughty 'hands off I hate you' airs that totally contradicted the way she responded to him.

His body remembered everything about her. The way she gave herself to him in a no-holds-barred way. Their lovemaking had been thrilling, electrifying and amazingly addictive. It had made him relax his 'three dates...four at the most' rule. It wasn't that he was a diehard playboy like some of his cousins; it just worked better for him to be free to move around without the ties and responsibilities of a committed relationship. But something about the coolly sophisticated Isabelle Harrington had made him relax those rules.

He had indulged himself in a four-week affair, kidding himself it would simultaneously end with her business studies. It was his get-out clause. The fact she got out first irked him. But rather than show her he was disappointed he'd let it slide. It wasn't as if he'd been ready to settle down at the age of twenty-four.

But it had been years before he forgot the scent of her signature fragrance and the silky feel of her hair against his skin. The feel of her soft mouth as she gave herself to him, the way her tongue shyly tangled with his, the way her teeth scraped along his jaw in little playful bites.

Flirting with her was entertaining. It made the blood tick in his veins. Excited him. Aroused him. But could he risk another affair with her? He was here to work. He had a punishing task ahead of him to convince his family he had what it took to make this takeover successful in every way possible. A fling with Isabelle Harrington could work against his goals. Distract him from them in a way he could well do without.

But then he remembered she'd said she had a boyfriend. Was it serious? How serious? Clearly not serious enough for her to have a ring on her left hand. Wasn't that the goal of every woman over thirty? Was she casually dating or committed? Was she in love or in lust? Why did he even care? It was none of his business who she saw. He had enough on his plate right now without adding Isabelle Harrington as a garnish.

His gaze took in the plush furnishings of his suite. Apart from the accessories Isabelle had strategically positioned, the suite was tastefully and elegantly decorated. Top-quality fabric for the festooned curtains and pelmets. Ankle-deep finely woven wool carpet on the floor. Italian polished marble in the bathroom with shiny brass and gold fittings. Antique furniture, crystal chandeliers, wall lights and table lamps that gave the suite the atmosphere of Old Money and class. The sort of place the super-wealthy came to in order to retreat from the frantic pace of the modern world. It was like stepping back in time, to an era when service was personalised and respectful, not generic and resentful as in some of the larger chain hotels. Choosing staff that perfectly reflected a hotel's mission statement was paramount and it was something Spencer wanted to discuss with Isabelle.

In his discussion with Liliana earlier he had found out Isabelle had personally interviewed the front-of-house staff. She had high standards and expected total commitment from the people who worked at The Harrington. She surrounded herself with people she could rely on to maintain the respectable and sophisticated reputation of the hotel. No one could ever question she wasn't dedicated and driven and yet he couldn't help feeling she was using her career as a shield. Hiding behind it like a suit of armour, not allowing anyone close enough to see the warm passionate woman behind the cool and distant professional façade.

Spencer picked up the velvet mask she had placed on his pillow. A flicker of remorse beat like moth wings trapped inside the chamber of his heart. He hadn't exactly charmed her to his side with how he'd gone about things. He could blame her wastrel brother but Spencer knew he had to accept some responsibility for how things had panned out. Maybe he should have called her and asked for a meeting before he'd come in with the takeover bid. Even if she'd rejected the offer at least it would have shown he was prepared to negotiate with her. Maybe he should have apologised years ago for how things had ended between them.

Maybe he should have told her...what? That he'd fallen for her? Like that was going to happen. He didn't know if he would recognise love if it whopped him on the head. He had never fallen for anyone. He wasn't sure he was capable of that once-in-a-lifetime love novelists and filmmakers portrayed. He didn't trust his emotions given how they had let him down in the past. He had loved his parents only to find one of them wasn't his own flesh and blood.

How could he ever trust anything or anyone after that?

He put down the velvet mask and looked at the mirror on the ceiling and on the wall at the foot of the bed. Isabelle had gone to a lot of trouble to remind him of what she thought of him—a time-wasting playboy who was just playing at hotels. She had no idea of the drive that motivated him. It wasn't about money. It wasn't about prestige. It wasn't even about his reputation because that was one thing that had never concerned him. He didn't care a fig what the press said about him personally. Most of the time they made up stuff to drum up sales. He went along with it. Mostly. He didn't court scandal but neither did he actively avoid it. If it happened it happened. But his professional reputation was a different matter entirely. His motto was Results Speak. No one could argue with numbers. If he could take The Harrington to the top of the boutique market in New York, then maybe he would be satisfied.

Finally.

Isabelle printed off a list of ideas she had for the ball, grinding her teeth as the printer spewed it out. She tucked it in a Harrington vellum folder and made her way to Spencer's office. It was well past five p.m. but she didn't care. He thought he could throw his weight around and she would jump out of the way. More fool him.

His door was closed but she could hear him talking to someone on the phone. She gave a brisk knock and then she heard footsteps and the door opened. He jerked his head against his phone and signalled for her to come in, continuing his conversation. 'How much damage are we talking about?' There was a small pause as the person on the other end of the line answered, and then he said, '*That* much? Who *are* these people? One hit record and they think they're gods? Get on to our lawyers. Slap these idiots with a damages suit. And get them out of there. Got it?'

He put the phone down on his desk and scraped a hand through his hair. 'What a bloody nightmare.'

Isabelle had never seen him so rattled. 'What's going on?'

His eyes collided with hers. 'A boy band—that new one that's just been launched off one of those reality talent shows—just trashed a suite at The Chatsfield, London. A hundred thousand pounds' worth of damage and still counting.'

She gripped the back of the chair in front of his desk. 'That's terrible.'

He gave her a black look. 'Tell me about it. I so don't need this right now.'

Isabelle pulled her lower lip inside her mouth. He so rarely showed his human side, the man behind the mask of steely control. The stress of his job as CEO of all the Chatsfield hotels was huge and it would have an effect on him even if he put steps in to guard against it. She had only seen him as the enemy, an obstacle to her goal. But he had an enormous responsibility to make sure everything ran smoothly and professionally. She understood that more than anyone. It was a daily pressure to keep everything under control. And while no one—no matter how dedicated and professional— could prepare for something like this, it still caused speculation about how well the hotel was being managed, which in turn would reflect on him. As newly appointed CEO, everyone would be looking for him to fall at the first hurdle.

Isabelle pulled away from her compassionate side. What did she care what happened to his professional reputation? The only thing she cared about was *her* hotel. Boy bands could trash every single one of the Chatsfield hotels and she wouldn't lose a wink of sleep over it.

'The press will make a huge thing about it, which will damage the brand we've worked so hard to improve,' he said. 'Who in their right mind would want to stay in a hotel where drunken orgies take place?'

'Groupies?'

His harsh frown softened and he even affected a twisted smile. 'Let me guess. You've downloaded all of their songs.'

'Not all of them. But I do have a favourite. I do my workout to it every morning.'

He narrowed his gaze in mock reproach. 'Do you have posters of them on your wall?'

She gave him a look. 'I'm not twelve.'

He put his hands on his desk in a bracing manner. 'What have you got for me?'

Isabelle slid the folder towards him. 'A black-and-blue theme or we could do black and pink. Black and white's been done to death. Hefty price tag all donated to charity.'

'Which charity?'

'Do you have a favourite?'

He drummed his fingers on the desk as he glanced over her proposal. 'Too many to count.'

'What's closest to your heart?'

He looked up at that and meshed his gaze with hers. 'What's yours?'

'I asked you first.'

He held her look for a beat before looking back at her proposal. 'Kids.'

A sharp stabbing pain caught her under the ribs. If her little baby had gone to term she would be nine years old. Isabelle could picture her in her mind—a skinny, leggy little girl with dark hair and blue eyes. Would she have been intense and uptight like her or laid-back and casual like her father? Would her smile be tentative like hers or enigmatic like Spencer's? She thought of Spencer holding their baby as she had so longed to do but was cruelly robbed of the chance. She thought of him playing with their little girl as a toddler, walking her into school on the first day. Helping her with her homework, teaching her how to ride a bike. All the things good fathers did with their daughters.

Would he have loved their little girl even half as much as Isabelle had loved her? Would he have wanted her as she had grown to want her?

What was she doing?

She didn't allow herself to think about babies and toddlers. Not anymore. It was a no-go area in her head. It was a barred zone in her heart. 'Kids?'

He gave her a wry look. 'You think I don't like kids?'

'You're a playboy. I thought the general idea was to avoid making them.'

'I don't want to *make* them.' His stress on the word made Isabelle's stomach twist into a painful knot. 'But I do like to help them. Especially disadvantaged ones.'

'That's...er...noble of you.'

He crooked a dark eyebrow at her. 'You don't see me as a philanthropist?'

'It's not something you've made public.'

'I've always found I can get more done if I fly under the radar,' he said. 'Kids don't buy into the rich celebrity stuff. Not the kids I work with anyway.'

Isabelle frowned in surprise. 'You work with them? In what way?'

'Teaching them life skills, confidence-building exercises, sporting programmes—that sort of thing. Even kids from wealthy backgrounds can lose their way. Become displaced and act out. My charity works on nipping that sort of behaviour in the bud. We redirect the negative energy into more positive outlets.'

Isabelle wondered what it was about his childhood that made him so motivated to help others in such an honourable way. He came from a good family, a seemingly stable family, unlike that of his cousins. At least his mother, Emily, and his father, Michael, had stayed together as they'd raised their three boys. Ben and James were now settled, Ben with her baby sister Olivia, and James with Princess Leila of Surhaadi. There was just Spencer who was footloose. What did he want for his life? Was he truly happy with the fly-by-night pattern he had adopted over the years? Or was he like her? Driven to succeed with little time to think of anything but work?

'Right, well, I thought we could do a silent auction as well,' she said. 'With big-ticket items such as a portrait done by a famous artist or a sculpture. What do you think?'

He looked up from her notes as if he had forgotten she was there. 'Sounds good.'

Isabelle frowned. 'Is something wrong? Apart from the London stuff, I mean? Do you need to fly back home?'

His mouth slanted. 'That would suit you down to the ground, wouldn't it? I wonder what sort of mischief you'd get up to while I was out of town?'

She gave him a defiant look. 'I can assure you I wouldn't wait until you were out of sight if I wanted to get up to mischief. I would do it in your face.'

He gave a sudden grin. 'You would indeed.' He waited a beat before adding, 'What are you doing for dinner?'

She blinked to reorient herself after the stun-gun effects of his disarming grin. 'Pardon?'

'We could discuss the ball over a meal. Fine-tune the details.'

She elevated her chin. 'I have a date.'

'Anyone I know?'

'No.'

'What's he do?'

Isabelle arched an eyebrow. 'Would you like me to email you a copy of his CV? Get a printout of his birth certificate, his vital statistics, his waist measurement and shoe size, the length of his—'

'How long have you been seeing him?'

'My private life is out of bounds.'

'Is it serious?'

Isabelle narrowed her gaze. 'Did you hear me?'

'Don't forget about our weekend.'

'I'm not going with you.'

'You can bring lover boy,' he said. 'Or wouldn't he like sharing you with me?'

She turned on her heel and stalked to the door. 'I'm not having this conversation.'

'If he doesn't work out for you let me know.'

She turned and gave him a contemptuous glare. 'Do you really think I'd subject myself to being used by you for a second time?'

Something moved in his expression—a sudden tension in his jaw, a flash of irritation in his eyes—before he just as quickly masked it. 'We could use each other,' he said. 'Scratch that itch we both feel around each other.'

Isabelle forced herself to hold his all-seeing gaze. 'I don't know what you're talking about.'

He gave a low deep laugh. 'Sure you do. You remember it all, don't you, darling? That's why you blush when I look at you a certain way. You remember how it felt to have me full to the hilt inside you while you thrashed and screamed—'

'Stop it!' Isabelle clamped her hands over her ears. 'Stop it, damn you!'

He pulled her hands down and encircled her wrists with his long strong fingers, his eyes blazing with the sensual heat she could feel engulfing her body. Desire ran red-hot inside her, like a lick of flame following a trail of fuel, his incendiary words triggering everything that was wickedly primitive in her. She could feel the hard wall of his body against her breasts, the erotic proximity—the temptation—suddenly too much to bear. Her pride got shoved sideways as she pushed up on her toes to meet his mouth halfway.

The collision of her lips against his was like an explosion inside her body. The first stroke of his tongue as it sought for entry to her mouth caused her knees to buckle. She would have fallen except his hands had left her wrists and were now on her hips, holding her so tightly against his pelvis she could feel the hard male imprint of his body against hers. It fuelled her hunger for him, ramping it up to a level that made her feel she would *die* if he didn't possess her. Her insides contracted with need, seeped and wept and wailed with want, throbbing with an ache that was escalating with every commanding stab and thrust of his tongue as it sought to conquer hers.

Her hands went to the front of his shirt, her nails digging in for purchase as she fused her mouth to his in a ravenous consumption of the sensual delights he offered. He tasted of coffee and mint and something else unique to him. Her mouth remembered it like a favourite wine. She was drunk on it. A helpless slave to it. Addicted to it like a potent drug. One taste and it had the same unbreakable hold on her it'd had in the past. She feasted off his lips and tongue, playing cat-and-mouse and catch-me-if-you-can and tease-me-and-tame-me.

His hands moved from her hips to skim up her body to graze over her breasts. It was the lightest touch as if he was testing her response to him but it was as if he had set fire to her flesh. Her breasts swelled beneath her clothes, her nipples tightening so much she could feel them against the lace cage of her bra. She slipped her hands through the gaps between his shirt buttons, not even caring that two of them popped off and pinged to the floor. His chest was hard and hot and with just the right smattering of masculine hair to make everything that was feminine in her shiver and shake and shudder and scream in want.

His fingers splayed through her hair as he played with her lips with his teeth in nibbling bites that made her whimper in breathless approval. He had always known just how hard or soft he could go with her—that delicate balance between pleasure and pain. He read her—*played her*—like a maestro did a complicated instrument. He had an intuitive sense of her needs even before she recognised or acknowledged them herself. That was perhaps the most unsettling thing about having him back in her life. He *knew* her. He knew the passionate wanton he had awakened a decade ago. She had wrestled that part of herself and locked it away, caging it like a wild animal not safe to be let loose. Now he had unpicked the lock, and who knew the damage that could do...

'Told you this was dangerous,' he said against her lips. 'Want it here or upstairs?'

Isabelle stiffened as if frozen. Had he read her mind? *What was she doing?* Hadn't she learned her lesson? This was a game to him. He had set out to prove a point and she had fallen for it.

But there was a way she could get the upper hand. She forced herself to relax, leaning into his aroused body, even going so far as to rub against him suggestively as her lips played against his. 'Give me half an hour.' She pressed another light teasing kiss to his mouth. 'I'll come to your suite. Someone might disturb us in here.'

His eyes glittered with raw desire and something else equally dangerous. 'Make it an hour. It'll be worth the wait. I guarantee it.'

CHAPTER FOUR

ISABELLE DRESSED IN a conservative little black dress with a scarlet silk wrap she draped around her shoulders. Her get-to-know-you drink with the man from the social media dating app had agreed to meet her in The Harrington bar. She figured it would serve two ends: it was a safe place to meet a stranger, and she would be sending Spencer a clear message that he couldn't have her just for the asking. That she wanted him was immaterial. She would not allow herself to want him. She would discipline herself not to want him. If it took every ounce of energy she possessed she *would* resist him.

There was no sign of her date when she entered the bar so she took one of the comfortable wing chairs in the more private section and ordered a champagne cocktail.

The head bartender, Carlos, came over with her drink. 'Good evening, Miss Harrington.' He glanced at the empty chair opposite hers. 'Will I order a drink for Mr Chatsfield?'

Isabelle frowned. 'I'm not meeting Mr Chatsfield. I'm meeting a…a friend.'

'Oh, my mistake,' Carlos said. 'Ah, there he is now with his date.'

His date?

Isabelle swivelled in her chair to see Spencer walk in with a stunning blonde on his arm. The girl looked like she was barely out of her teens. She was slim to the point of thin, with long coltish legs that were spray tanned a gorgeous honey brown, and she was wearing such high heels her hips swayed with every step she took.

Isabelle felt something bitter like acid spill inside her stomach. *Well, two could play at that game.* Just wait until *her* date showed up. She crossed her legs and sipped her cocktail and waited.

And waited.

And watched as Spencer Chatsfield chatted to the blonde at the other end of the bar area. He hadn't even glanced Isabelle's way. It was as if she were invisible. He only had eyes for the gorgeous model-like goddess perched on one of the brass-stemmed stools.

Isabelle dragged her gaze away and scrolled through her emails. Read a few Twitter posts. Made a few inane comments on some friends' pages on Facebook. Then finally her phone beeped with a message. It was probably her date saying he was caught up in traffic or on the subway or something, she thought. She clicked on the message icon. Date not show up? Spencer.

Isabelle glared at him from across the room. He lifted a hand in a casual wave and then returned his attention to the vision of loveliness beside him. Isabelle ground her teeth, her stomach burning and churning as the girl trailed a talon-like fingertip around his mouth. The mouth that only an hour ago *she* had been kissing.

Her phone beeped again. This time it was the man from the dating app saying he'd changed his mind about meeting. She didn't know whether to be relieved or disappointed. The worst of it was she now had to sit and watch Spencer flirt with his young date unless she left, thus showing him she had in fact been stood up.

Carlos came over with another cocktail. 'Compliments of Mr Chatsfield.'

Isabelle wished she could have told him to throw it in Spencer's face. She gritted her teeth behind a polite smile. 'Thank him, will you?'

She drank the cocktail with a little more haste than usual. Her head started to spin but then every tense muscle in her body began to relax. So what if her date hadn't shown up? She could still have a good time. She might still get lucky. Show Spencer he wasn't the only one who could pull a date. There were plenty of good-looking men coming into the bar, and not all of them were partnered like he was. She caught sight of one looking at her from across the room. He wasn't as tall as Spencer and he was carrying a little more weight but he had a nice smile.

He came over to her. 'Hi, there. I saw you sitting here all on your own. Can I get you a drink?'

'Sure,' Isabelle said, smiling back. 'I'll have a champagne cocktail.'

'No, she won't,' Spencer said, suddenly appearing beside her chair. 'Darling, do you really think you should be drinking alcohol in your condition?'

The man stepped back as if he'd been slapped, his cheeks going a dull red. 'I didn't realise you two were together.'

'We're not—'

'Telling anyone until it's official,' Spencer cut her off neatly.

'Congratulations...' The man looked a little bewildered and more than a little intimidated by Spencer's towering presence. 'Look, I'm really sorry if I offended you. She was sitting over here by herself and I thought...'

'No problem.' Spencer was all Chatsfield charm. 'I shouldn't have left her all alone. She always gets into mischief when I turn my back, don't you, darling?'

'But that's what you love about me, isn't it, honey pie?' Isabelle said with a simpering look while inside she was boiling with rage. 'You never know what to expect next.'

How could he *joke* about something so serious? Even though he had no idea of the hurt he was causing, she hated him all over again for being so unspeakably cruel. The nerve-scraping pain travelled from the deep well inside her, threatening to overwhelm her. Her loss, her guilt, her shattered hopes—the whole confusing mix swirling around inside her head, pressing on her heart like the weight of an anchor, churning in her stomach in acidic waves. She fought to contain herself, to gather her spiralling emotions. She could not—*would not*—break down in front of Spencer. She would not allow him the power to dismantle her, to reduce her to a weeping, snivelling, shattered mess.

The man slinked away and Spencer's charming smile was quickly exchanged for a savage frown. 'What the hell do you think you were doing?' he said.

Isabelle glared at him, her voice lowered to a hiss. 'Are you out of your mind? You told that guy I was—' she swallowed before she could get the word past the choking knot in her throat '—pregnant.'

'At no point did I say the word *pregnant*.'

Her throat was raw from holding back a wellspring of bitterness and pain. She could barely breathe for the suffocating ache pressing against her chest. 'You implied it, then. What if he tells someone? What if he knows who we are? It'll be all over the press or social media before—'

'Since when do you go picking up strangers in a bar?' His frown was so deep it created a crevasse between his eyes.

Isabelle lifted her eyebrows in an arch. 'What about you coming in with that girl you picked up from the nearest child-minding centre?'

He gave her a hardened look. 'Very funny.'

'Who is she?'

'No one special.'

She made a huffing sound. 'No one is special to you, are they? You just pick them up and drop them when it suits you.'

He took her by the hand. 'Come on. Let's get out of here. The staff are watching.'

Isabelle tried to pull against his hold but his fingers were so firm they felt like an iron clamp. But rather than cause a scene she had no choice but to leave with him. She adopted a cool and poised posture as if there was nothing unusual about him leading her out of the bar towards his office.

He opened the door and ushered her through, closing it behind him with a firm snick. 'I thought you said you had a boyfriend.'

Isabelle held her chin at a haughty height. 'I was supposed to be meeting someone but they cancelled at the last minute. I thought I'd take a leaf out of your book and see what fate dished up instead.'

His eyes were so dark she could barely make out his pupils. 'Who were you supposed to be meeting?'

She pinched her lips together. Folded her arms. Defied him with a stare-down look. Anger was good. She could deal with anger. It was sadness and regret and grief that ambushed and confused her.

He stepped up to her and took her by the upper arms. 'Tell me, damn it.'

Isabelle winced even though his touch electrified rather than hurt. 'Ouch! You're hurting me.'

His hold instantly softened but he didn't release her. His dark blue gaze was intensely focused on hers, his mouth set in a firm line. 'You don't have a regular boyfriend, do you?'

Her cheeks heated as she tried to out-stare him. How galling to have to admit her singleton status. To admit she didn't have anyone in her life who wanted her. 'I fail to see how that's any business of yours.'

His fingers moved in a gently massaging manner on her upper arms, his thumbs in particular stroking the inside of her arms near her armpits, a sensitive area she'd forgotten she'd possessed until he reclaimed it with his mesmerising touch. 'I'm making it my business.'

She jutted her chin. 'Why?'

'Because I'm not going to stand by and watch you hook up with someone just to prove a point,' he said. 'If you want to hook up with someone, then you can damn well hook up with me.'

Isabelle gave a choked laugh. 'You think I'm *that* desperate?'

'No,' he said, and tightened his hold as he drew her closer as his mouth came down towards hers. 'But *I* am.'

It was a hot searching kiss. A kiss of longing and yearning and frustration and maybe even a little bit of anger thrown in too. Isabelle didn't fight it. Didn't dream of fighting it. She could do this. She could have mindless sex without feeling anything for him. It was what was lacking in her life. Passion. Adventure. Excitement. Satisfaction.

But this time she would have him on *her* terms.

She was as hungry for his mouth as he was for hers. She succoured on it, savouring his taste like imbibing a prohibited drink. She was heady on it, her mind and her senses spinning in delight as he deepened the kiss with a thrust of his tongue that mimicked the red-hot desire she could feel in his body where it was jammed up against hers.

His jaw was prickly against hers as he repositioned to explore her mouth in further depth. She surrendered to it, taking him in and playing with him in a dance that was eons old. He made a sound of approval, a deep groan-like murmur that made her insides shiver in recognition. Oh, how she *loved* that sound! How many times over the past decade had she thought of that utterly male sound, the way it reverberated in his chest where it was pressed against hers? The way it signalled the need that pulsed and throbbed in his body as it pulsed and throbbed in hers. The way their bodies fitted together like two pieces of a complicated puzzle. There were no awkward angles or shuffles. It was pure magic, a complex and yet perfect choreography they alone knew and responded to intuitively.

His hands splayed through her hair, his mouth locked to hers as his tongue swept over and under hers in a lust-driven duel. She came back at him with the same level of daring, brazenly taking him deeper into her mouth, then sucking on him, tugging at him with her teeth, reminding him of the fire and passion that burned and bubbled like molten lava in her body.

Her hands went to his head, holding him down to her mouth by pressing on the back of his skull, her fingers delving into the lush thickness of his hair. He made another low deep sound and pulled her even closer, his hardness against her softness, want against want, need against need.

Isabelle gave a gasp as one of his hands deftly released the zipper at the back of her dress. It slipped to the floor leaving her in her bra and panties and heels. There was something so sexy, so wicked and risqué, about being in his office in just her underwear.

She reached for his zipper and slid it down and went in search of him. He muttered an expletive as her fingers wrapped around his hardened length. That was another sound she loved—the sound of a man who was pushed to the brink of control. No other man had ever made her feel quite so desirable. She could feel the pounding of his blood against her fingertips, the primal need to mate so intense in him it echoed the aching throb between her thighs.

No one aroused her like this man. No one made her ache with a need so frantic it totally consumed her. She could not think of anything but how it would feel to have him driving into her with that first deep blood-thickened thrust.

He went for the fastener on her bra, his hands skating over her breasts in a teasing touch that made her nipples tighten almost painfully. His mouth left hers to blaze a hot moist pathway to her breast but she was too impatient for him to dawdle there. She pushed her pelvis into his, urging him in breathless little mewling sounds to do what they were both here to do.

He held her back from him, looking down at her with lust-glazed eyes. 'You're in rather a hurry, aren't you?'

Isabelle gave him a sultry look. 'It's what you want, isn't it? A quickie on your big brand-new CEO desk?'

Something shifted in his gaze, his hold relaxing as if the tension was ebbing out of his body. 'Maybe this isn't the right time to do this.'

She cocked an eyebrow, refusing to acknowledge how much his drawing back disappointed her. 'I thought you wanted to scratch that itch?'

His lips moved in and out as if he were pondering over something. Then he dropped his hands from her waist and stepped back and zipped up his trousers. He pushed a hand backwards over his head, his hand stopping to rub at the back of his neck as if it was causing him discomfort. 'This doesn't feel right.'

Isabelle perched on the edge of his desk, crossing her legs and positioning herself with her arms braced behind her body to look like a high-class hooker paid to service him. 'Come and get me, English boy. I'm all yours.'

He tightened his mouth, a muscle moving in and out on the hinge of his jaw as if he were gritting his teeth. 'Put your clothes on.'

Isabelle raised her chin. '*You* took them off. *You* can put them back on.'

She saw his hands clench and unclench before he thrust them in his trouser pockets. It looked as if the biggest battle was with himself far more than it was with her. She could see it in the way he held himself: the set to his jaw, the flat line to his mouth, the squarely braced shoulders and the ramrod-straight spine. 'I'm not going to play your game, Isabelle.'

This was one skirmish Isabelle was determined to win. She wanted him to admit his need for her, if not verbally, then physically. It was the perfect payback, to have no-strings sex with him, a hot fling that had nothing whatsoever to do with emotion or intimacy or bonding. She would reduce him to his most primal. She would do whatever it took to get him to break. The challenge of it surged in her blood, making her reckless and daring in a way she had never realised she could be. It was as if a part of her personality she had always suppressed in the past was now out and ready to play.

She uncrossed her legs and brazenly spread them, hooking a finger inside one edge of her panties so he could see a tantalising little glimpse of what he was missing. 'Come on, Spencer.' Her voice was low and husky and breathy. 'You know you want to.'

She saw the steely control that was so tied up with his personality being bombarded by the way she was pushing him, goading him, teasing him. It gave her such a rush of power it was almost as exciting as the passion he had stirred just moments earlier.

His jaw was so tightly clamped his lips barely moved as he spoke. 'No.'

Isabelle arched her brow and tugged her panties a little further aside. 'You sure about that? I'm all wet and hot for you. Want to touch me and see?'

He sucked in a harsh breath but remained six feet away from her. Every muscle on his body was locked tight. He was like a marble statue, all except for his blazing eyes. 'Don't cheapen yourself.'

She laughed a throaty laugh. 'No, that's your job, isn't it?'

A dull flush rode high on his cheekbones. 'Why are you doing this?'

She blinked at him guilelessly; stretching back even further on her arms, her hair swinging to one side as she tilted her head at him. 'Why am I doing what?'

He let out a filthy curse and strode to the bank of windows that overlooked the New York skyline. His back was so rigid she could see every taut muscle straining beneath the fine cotton of his shirt. He lifted his hands to shoulder height and rested them on the panes of glass, his head hanging between them as he released a long breath. 'Get out.'

Isabelle casually rolled her top ankle where it was crossed over the other. 'I told you before. I won't take orders from you.'

His hands were pressing so hard upon the glass it was a wonder the panels didn't fall out to the street below. Every muscle in his arms was bunched so tightly they, too, looked as if they might burst out of the restraints of his shirtsleeves. 'I'm warning you, Isabelle.' His voice contained a thread of steel that made her shiver in reaction. 'Get out before your little game backfires on you.'

Isabelle was getting so turned on by their war of wills she could feel the tingles of it in her core. He wanted her as badly as she wanted him. But like her, he refused to be seen as the one weakened by it, vulnerable because of it.

She slipped down off the desk and came towards

him. It was like approaching a tiger in a paper cage. Dangerous. Foolish. Reckless. Any moment he could spring at her but she couldn't stop herself from having one last poke at his self-control.

She trailed a fingertip down the length of his spine from the base of his neck to the small of his back. She felt him flinch. It reminded her of the way a stallion's coat quivers in order to shake off the brush of an annoying fly. She pressed herself against him, her breasts pushing against his shoulder blades. 'You sure you want me to leave?' she asked in a smoky whisper.

He drew in a sharp breath and turned, roughly fisting a hand in her hair while the other grasped her by the hip, his fingers digging in almost painfully. His eyes were a dark inky blue, the pupils wide and deep and bottomless with arousal. But his mouth remained in a cynical slant that belied everything his body was telling her. 'You think I can't resist you?'

Isabelle moved her pelvis against his, shamelessly rubbing her tingling mound against the swollen ridge of his erection. 'I bet right now if I got down on my knees I could make you come with just a couple of licks.'

His eyes combatted with hers for a long throbbing moment.

She could sense the erotic excitement in him. Her brazen promise had triggered something primitive and dangerous in him. The primal heat was thick and humid in the air. The atmosphere was electric, pulsing with sexual energy looking for an outlet.

She lowered her gaze to his mouth, licking her own lips to make them moist and inviting. 'How about it? You want to come in my mouth or over my breasts?'

His hands visibly shook as he set her from him.

His mouth was so tightly set his lips were a thin line of chalk-white. He walked over to the door of his office, his hand poised on the doorknob. 'I'm going to give you thirty seconds to get your gear on before I open this door.'

Isabelle knew she was beaten. He had cleverly won that round. There was no way she would risk having one of her staff see her standing there in her underwear. But she would have other opportunities.

And she would make the most of them.

She gave an easy-come-easy-go shrug and leaned down to pick up her dress. She stepped into it and wriggled it back into place, pulling her hair out of the way of the zipper as she slid it back up. She did it slowly, like a reverse striptease, lingering over every movement.

She picked up her wrap and draped it around her shoulders as she walked to the door he was about to open. She stood right in front of him, looking up into his closed-off features, giving him one last sultry look from beneath her half-mast lashes. 'If you change your mind you know where to find me.'

His eyes were as hard as flint as they clashed with hers. 'Is that what you do now? Just hang around in bars waiting to hook up with whoever takes your fancy?'

Isabelle gave him a mocking smile. 'Is that a double standard I can hear?'

He opened the door and stepped back so she could pass through. His body was as stiff as the door itself. A stonewall of fiercely repressed lust she could feel pulsating behind the mask of indifference he wore. Her body responded to it as she moved past him, every cell throbbingly aware of how he alone could satisfy the deepest yearning of her flesh.

She turned just as she was about to step over the threshold. 'About that weekend.'

'What about it?' The words were clipped, his tone dismissive.

Isabelle smiled a seductress's smile. 'You're right. Sharing a room makes good economic sense. Shall I leave you to make the arrangements?'

His jaw worked for a moment. 'You won't win this.'

She stroked a finger down the length of his still-hard erection. 'I think we can safely say I just did.'

CHAPTER FIVE

SPENCER SHUT THE DOOR on her. Slammed the door on his pounding desire. He would not play her petty little payback game. He would have her but on his terms, not hers. She was toying with him. Goading him. Reducing him to his animal desires to prove a point. He'd seen through it earlier when she'd told him she'd meet him in his room. He'd known she wasn't going to show. That's why he'd walked into the bar with the blonde on his arm to show Isabelle he wasn't going to be manipulated.

But this time was different.

She had offered herself to him like a hooker. And he had very nearly taken her up on the offer. Never had he been so close to losing control. He had almost disgraced himself as she teased him with those wickedly tempting words. He had been within a heartbeat of joining her on that desk. He raked a still-shaky hand through his hair. *Dear God. That desk.* He could barely look at the thing without another painful surge of want. His whole body ached with it. Throbbed with it. *Groaned* with it.

Why was she so determined to make him break? What did she hope to prove? That he wanted her more than she wanted him? They wanted each other. He could see it every time she looked at him. He could *feel* it. It was like electric voltage in the air. It pulsated with it. Vibrated with it. He felt it in his body when she touched him or he touched her. He saw it in her eyes, in the way her pupils dilated, in the way her gaze kept slipping to his mouth as if inviting him to devour the sweetness and hot temptation he had tasted there.

He swore as he paced the floor. He felt like a lion housed in a cat carrier. Was she doing it to deliberately distract him? She hated him for the takeover. What better way to manipulate him than to distract him from the task he had set himself? She had been distraction enough in the past, let alone now when so much more was at stake. How could he indulge himself in an affair with her when he had so many other pressures on him just now? Or was that what she wanted? To bring him down any way she could.

But if he didn't take up her offer of a fling someone else would. That was what niggled him. It irritated the hell out of him. How could he stand by and watch her throw herself away on any man who offered to bed her? How long had she been doing that? It was a side to her he hadn't expected. She was known for her poise and professionalism. It didn't suit her persona to be throwing herself at the first man who showed an interest. What was she doing picking up men in The Harrington bar, for God's sake? Surely she had a higher regard for the hotel, if not for herself, than that?

No. Something was wrong about this. *About her.* There was a streak of ruthlessness about her that alerted him to an agenda apart from her disappointment about the takeover.

The corners of his mouth lifted in a smile. Maybe it was time to call her bluff.

Isabelle was celebrating her one-upmanship win with a glass of champagne back in her suite. 'You should have seen him, Atticus,' she said to the purring cat on the sofa. 'He was so worked up I could have had him eating out of my hand.' She drained the glass and picked up the bottle to refill it. *You're drinking too much*, a little voice piped up, but she drowned it out with the sound of the bubbles dancing into the glass. 'He thinks he can resist me, does he? Ha!'

There was a knock on the door.

'That will be room service.' She glanced at her watch as she padded over to open it. 'Gosh, that was quick. I only just…'

Spencer looked at the glass in her hand before returning his gaze to her shocked one. 'What are we celebrating?'

Isabelle swallowed. 'What are you doing here?'

One of his dark brows lifted. 'You invited me, remember?'

She bit the inside of her mouth. Atticus was lying on the sofa. In her half-tipsy state she hadn't thought to put him in the bedroom as she usually did when someone came to the door. Only a handful of trusted staff knew she had him. If Spencer found out about him he might insist she get rid of him. It was exactly the sort of thing he would do to punish her. 'I'm busy right now,' she said, leaning her weight against the door to stop him coming in.

He had already put a foot in the gap to stop her closing it, his eyes locking on hers. 'Surely not too busy to talk to me?'

Isabelle tested the strength he was putting against the door. She had no hope of blocking him from entering. But then, wasn't that her problem? She wanted him inside and she wasn't just referring to her suite. Her desire for him was already unfolding, stretching its limbs inside her. It was a force she had no control over. Her body had its own agenda and she was at its mercy. 'I'm not in the mood to talk.'

'Good because nor am I.'

A frisson of excitement passed through her body at the dark intensity of his gaze. She had to get rid of him even though every cell in her being was clamouring for him. 'You can't come in right now,' she said.

'Is someone with you?'

She raised her chin a fraction. 'Yes.'

Something ticked near his mouth. 'Male?'

'Yes.'

His eyes battled with hers. 'I don't believe you.'

Isabelle affected a disparaging laugh. 'You don't think I could pick up a date that quickly?'

The look he gave her made something at the base of her spine work loose. 'Open the door.'

'You were ordering me out of your office half an hour ago,' she said. 'Now you expect me to invite you in? Sorry but the offer's been withdrawn.'

Isabelle heard the soft thump of Atticus as he jumped off the sofa. Even though the suite was carpeted the sound was deafening.

Spencer glanced past her shoulder. 'What was that?'

'Nothing.' Her heartbeat escalated. Any moment now Atticus would appear around the corner. He always came in search of her if she lingered too long at the door. 'Please leave me alone. I—I have a headache.'

'I'm not surprised given the amount of alcohol you've consumed.' He suddenly frowned as he glanced down where Atticus was winding his way around her legs. 'You've got a *cat*?'

Atticus looked up at him and mewed. *'Purrht.'*

'So?' Isabelle let go of the door and scooped up Atticus and glared at Spencer over the top of his fluffy head. 'What of it?'

'For God's sake, this is a hotel not a bloody pet shelter.' He closed the door with a snap. 'What else have you got hiding in here?'

She thought of the ultrasound image tucked in between the pages of her favourite book of poems on the bookshelf. 'Nothing.'

He nailed her with a look. 'Sure?'

She returned his gaze with steely focus. *Don't blush. Don't blush. Don't blush.* 'What's wrong with having a cat? He's not doing anyone any harm. It's not as if he has the run of the hotel. He never leaves my suite.'

He was still frowning. 'But cats are meant to be outdoors...or at least some of the time.'

'Not necessarily,' Isabelle said. 'Some prefer to be indoors. That's why they make such great pets. Unlike dogs they don't need a walk. They just need a bit of grooming.' A lot of grooming but she wasn't going to get into that right now.

'No way am I allowing this,' he said. 'Think of the health issues. This is a legal minefield. What if a guest gets toxoplasmosis or salmonella or campylobacter, to name just a few?'

Isabelle stroked Atticus's head. 'I'll have you know

my cat is perfectly healthy and doesn't have any horrible diseases.'

Spencer's frown was a deep trench between his eyes. 'I don't care how healthy he is you have to get rid of him or else.'

Her spine went broomstick stiff. 'Or else what?'

His jaw was set in an intractable line. 'I'll fire you.'

'You can't fire me,' she shot back. 'Liliana said her giving you the shares was provisional on my remaining president.'

His gaze bored into hers. 'Does she know about the cat?'

Isabelle's heart skipped a beat. She tried desperately not to squirm under his tight scrutiny. She didn't want to show him how vulnerable his ultimatum made her feel. Atticus was all she had. He was her companion. He was her substitute baby. The one thing she could nurture. The only thing she could nurture...would allow herself to nurture.

'I asked you a question.' There was a thread of steel in his tone.

'Lots of hotels allow pets,' she said. 'Hotels all over the States have heaps of them that—'

'I don't care what other hotels do,' he said. 'This one does not allow pets. No dogs. No cats. No birds. No hamsters. Do I make myself clear?'

Isabelle spun around to take Atticus back to the sofa. She placed him against his favourite scatter cushion and turned to face Spencer, who had followed her. 'This is the only home he's known,' she said. 'I've had him since he was six weeks old. You can't possibly expect me to get rid of him. It's cruel of you to even suggest it.'

He stood looking down at her for a beat or two. 'What do you do with him when you go on holiday?'

She rolled her lips together and looked away. 'I don't go on holiday much. I prefer to work.'

He came over to her and lifted her chin with his fingertip, his eyes searching hers. 'Who else knows you've got him?'

'A couple of the staff.'

He dropped his hand from her face, still looking at her with a thoughtful expression. 'Why a cat?'

'You don't like cats.' It was a statement not a question.

'I didn't say that.'

'I can see it by the way you looked at him,' she said. 'You think he's ugly.'

He gave a wry-sounding snort. 'Well, he does have the sort of face only a mother could love.'

Isabelle bit down on her lip and turned away again. The word *mother* always struck at her like a blow to the heart. She had never been able to decide if she qualified for the word. She had given birth to a dead baby. It wasn't even a full-term baby. Did that make her a mother? Every Mother's Day was a double form of torture to her now. Not only did she have no mother to celebrate it with, she didn't qualify to celebrate it herself. Every time she saw a mother pushing a child in a pram she felt the pain of her loss like a kick to her stomach. She picked up the champagne bottle with a hand that wasn't quite steady and refilled her glass. 'Would you like a drink?'

'Do you normally drink bottles of champagne all on your own?'

Isabelle sent him a defiant look. 'I'm not on my own. I've got Atticus.'

Spencer sighed heavily. 'I guess if I drink one glass it's one less you can consume.'

She poured him a glass and handed it to him. 'I'm not a binge drinker if that's what you're thinking.'

He took the glass but kept his gaze trained on hers. 'So what was with the hooker routine in my office?'

Isabelle swung away from him again, almost spilling her drink as she drew her arms in close to her body. 'You were after sex. I was going to give it to you.'

'It seems to me you were going to give it to anybody.'

She glanced at his frowning expression. 'Why did you refuse?'

He held her look for a pulsing moment, a rueful twist contorting the line of his mouth. 'I'm still kicking myself over that.'

Isabelle put her glass down and pressed her hands down her thighs. 'Yes, well, I was probably a bit tipsy. You were perfectly right to refuse. Shows what a gentleman you are.'

He put a hand on her shoulder and spun her to face him. 'I'm no gentleman.'

She looked into his dark blue eyes and felt her insides quake with lust. His hand was heavy on her shoulder, the fingers possessive in their grip. The warmth of his hand seeped through every layer of her flesh, triggering a flashpoint of heat deep in her core. 'I don't think this is a good idea right now...' she faltered. 'I'm tired and I've had too much champagne and you're...'

'I'm what?'

She swallowed and all but whispered, 'You're hard to resist when I'm…feeling—' dare she admit it? '—lonely…'

His hand went to the back of her head to the sensitive nape of her neck. She shivered as his touch awoke every ache of longing she secretly harboured for him. It was impossible to disguise her reaction to him. She heard herself whimper, the soft sound of that-feels-so-good-don't-stop that was the biggest betrayal of all. His hand kept up its gentle massage; it was a committed lover's touch, not the action of a transitory one-night stand. That was what was so hard for her to resist. The way he knew her body so well even though so much time had passed. That he could sense the need in her, the need to connect with another human. *To feel.* To feel alive and wanted, desired to the point of desperation. No one but him made her feel that way. It was as if he was the only one who knew who she truly was—the passionate woman behind the icy exterior, the woman who craved intimacy and tenderness and excitement and heart-stopping passion and everything else in between.

'Look at me,' he said.

She looked into his eyes. Saw the want, the raw need, reflected there that she could feel throbbing in her own body. 'I don't want to feel like this. I don't want to want you. I hate myself for it. I hate *you* for it.'

His smile twisted a little further as he brushed his thumb over her lower lip in a stroking motion. 'Maybe we should channel all that hate into another direction.'

Isabelle held her breath as he brought his mouth down towards hers. She didn't wait for him to complete the distance. She stepped up on her toes and meshed her mouth with his. It was not an explosion this time, more of a mutual exploratory exercise, a gentle, almost tender journey of rediscovery. His lips moved against hers, soft at first, then with increasing pressure. His tongue sought entry and she opened to him on a sigh she felt move through her entire body, loosening everything that was strung up and tight within her. She relaxed into his arms as they gathered her close, her pelvis fitting against the hardness of his like two puzzle pieces that had been missing for a long time.

His tongue grazed hers, teasing hers into playing with him, dancing and flirting until she was breathless with excitement. No one kissed as expertly as he did, as if he knew her mouth better than anyone else: its contours, its sensitivity, its need to be cajoled rather than conquered. His mouth made every part of her come alive like something awakening after a decade-long hibernation. All of her senses responded to the dart and dive of his tongue as it flirted with hers.

He spread his hands through her hair, making every strand shiver at the roots as he angled his head to deepen the kiss. She linked her arms around his neck, using her fingers to tug and tease the strands of his hair in the way she knew he liked. He made a deep sound of approval and pulled her closer, so close she felt the turgid length of him pressing against her belly. It excited her senses into a madcap frenzy. To feel him so ready, so primed and potent, made everything that was female in her quiver in heady anticipation.

He slid his hands down the sides of her body, his fingers just missing her breasts. He brought them back up, this time teasing her with the hint of a touch on the way past. She moved against his hips, communicating her need for him without words because she was beyond speaking. She was a slave to her senses. *His* slave.

She grabbed one of his hands as he repeated his tantalising journey down her body and brought it to her breast, pressing it to her so he could feel the bud of her nipple through the fabric of her clothes. His mouth kept feeding off hers, the deep sounds he was making telling her all she needed to know about how much he wanted her.

But then he gradually eased back from her, holding her by the upper arms as his gaze held hers, his expression twisted with ruefulness. 'Maybe I'm more of a gentleman than I realised.'

Isabelle felt the sting of rejection all over again. It bruised her ego, mocked her sense of power over him. Crucified her confidence. 'You don't want me?' She mentally kicked herself for sounding so needy. So disappointed. So vulnerable.

He drew in a breath and slowly released it. 'I'd hate myself in the morning if I took advantage of you like this.'

She gave a choked laugh. 'That didn't stop you ten years ago.'

Something in his expression flinched, like a tiny muscle close to his left eye was being tugged beneath the skin. 'I didn't ply you with alcohol to get you into bed. I seem to remember you came quite willingly.'

Isabelle compressed her lips and turned away, crisscrossing her arms over her body. She was walking a fine line. She was tipsy and emotional. She wasn't in control. She didn't want to be reminded of how keen she had been in the past. Even though she had played hard to get at first, it hadn't taken long for her to fall for his charm. Every moment she spent with him had seen her swept up into a world of romantic enchantment unlike anything she had encountered before, other than in a fairy tale. He had set about romancing her. It hadn't felt like a seduction at all. It had felt as if he was falling in love with her.

Oh, how annoyed she was with herself for falling for it! It was her biggest bugbear. That she had been so naive, so ripe for the picking in her quest for a happy-ever-after she hadn't seen how she was being played.

He hadn't wanted her. Her body yes, but not *her*. She'd been a challenge. A quest. A mission. She'd been nothing to him, just a silly little trophy to collect, like a cheap holiday souvenir.

How could she not have seen through it? No man had shown much interest in her before then. Her cool standoffishness had always left her on the fringe. Her introverted nature made connecting with others difficult, awkward even. Unless she could talk about work she was lost for words. She was hopeless at small talk, hopeless at being the life of the party. To find someone like Spencer Chatsfield seemingly captivated by her had fed her ego. It had made her swell and blossom with pride that a man of his sophistication, of his education and background, was so intent on pursuing her.

Why, oh, why hadn't she realised he hadn't be genuine?

'I'd like you to leave,' she said through tight lips.

'Not until I'm sure you're all right.'

She faced him again. Defiantly. Proudly. Recklessly. He was looking at her with a stern expression like a parent does at a disobedient teenager. The planes and contours of his handsome face set in implacable lines.

Why did he have to be so gallant all of a sudden? It was much easier to hate him when he was playing true to form. This was a side to him she hadn't met since they had dated ten years ago. A protective side she found disturbingly attractive. 'What are you going to do, Spencer? Tuck me into bed as if I'm five years old?'

He made an impatient sound through his nose. 'Have you eaten?'

She wandered over to lift the champagne bottle out of the ice bucket. 'I never drink on a full stomach,' she said, giving him a deliberately cheeky look. 'It spoils the fun.'

He was beside her before she could refill her glass. He took the bottle from her and ruthlessly upended it into the ice bucket. Isabelle didn't fight him over it. She hadn't intended drinking any more anyway. She stood with her arms folded, her mouth pushed out in a pout. 'Spoilsport.'

His brows were jammed together over his eyes. 'I never took you for a lush.'

She shrugged as if she didn't care what he thought of her. 'You think you know me but you don't.'

'Tell me why you're doing this to yourself.' His tone had gentled, his expression softened, no longer in harsh lines of disapproval or censure.

Isabelle could handle him when he was fighting with her…when he was angry with her. But this compassionate side was something that ambushed her defences. She didn't want to like him. She didn't want to respect him. She wanted to hate him. She *needed* to hate him, otherwise he would unravel her tightly bound emotions. She could not allow him close. To see the needs she had hidden for so long. She had to stay strong and invincible.

She tucked her hair back over her left shoulder with a sweep of her hand. 'Please leave. I don't want to talk to you right now.'

'This isn't just about the takeover, is it?'

She rolled her eyes as she turned away. 'As if *that* wasn't enough.'

He came up behind her and planted his hands on the tops of her shoulders. It was a gentle anchoring touch that made her want to lean back against him for the support she secretly, desperately craved.

But what if he had another agenda? What if he was only coming in close to exploit her further? Hadn't he exploited her enough? He would woo her to his side, make her say and do things she might later regret. He might wangle her out of even more shares.

Isabelle knew her tongue was dangerously loosened by the champagne she'd drunk. *Champagne?* How ironic. It was the drink of toasts and celebrations, and yet, what had she to celebrate? Her beloved hotel was no longer hers. Her life was being taken over by a man she didn't know how to handle. Had never known how to handle. He was too powerful. Too sophisticated. Too everything.

She held herself stiffly as she turned. Freezing him out with her gaze even though everything in her ached to feel his arms go around her and gather her close. 'You know you could've really cashed in on that bet if I'd told you the truth about me.'

He frowned at her in puzzlement. 'What truth about you?'

Fuelled by recklessness she knew she would probably regret later she said. 'How high would the stakes have gone up if you'd known I was a virgin?'

His eyes flared in shock, his face draining of colour, and his whole body tensing as if turned to stone. *'What?'*

Isabelle dipped out from under his hold and brushed past him to put some distance between them. She didn't trust herself not to reach for him, to lose herself in him. She had lost herself in him before. She couldn't risk it again. 'I wasn't quite the girl-about-town I led you to believe,' she said.

'Why didn't you say something?' His voice was deep and raw and gravelly. 'For God's sake, I could've hurt you.' He swallowed convulsively and added, *'Did I?'*

'No.'

He scraped a hand through his hair. Swallowed again. Looked at her with a pained expression. 'Are you sure?'

Isabelle affected a little laugh. 'All those riding lessons my parents insisted I take when I was a child finally paid off.'

He was still frowning at her like a reproachful parent. 'This is no laughing matter, Isabelle. You must know I would never have slept with you if I'd known.'

She gave him a pointed look. 'What about the bet?'

His jaw locked for a moment before he let out a harsh-sounding rush of air. He dragged a hand down his face from his forehead to his chin, letting it hang uselessly by his side in a gesture of resignation. 'I wasn't responsible for that.'

Isabelle wouldn't have believed him if he'd said that ten years ago but for some reason she did now. The

gravitas of his tone, the flicker of pain in his gaze before it moved away from hers, made her believe his
confession was genuine. He moved to the other side
of the room to stand in front of the windows. He had
done the same in his office. She wondered if it was
his way of gathering himself. Collecting his thoughts
and feelings so he didn't do or say anything he would
later regret.

The silence stretched for endless moments.

She saw him brace himself to speak. His back and
shoulders tightened before he turned to face her. 'It
was something two of my friends set up between themselves. I didn't hear about it until just before you did.'

'Then why not tell me?'

His expression had a shuttered look about it. 'I figured you'd be moving back to New York in a few weeks
so what was the point? We both knew our relationship
had a use-by date.'

Did we?

Isabelle felt the familiar stab of pain at his cavalier
approach to what they'd shared. He had reduced their
relationship to a cheap fling. A throwaway item that
wouldn't be missed once it was gone. She had invested
all of herself in their relationship. She had built her
dreams on the foundation of it. A foundation she later
found to be false—a joke between mates.

So what if he hadn't been the one responsible for
that stupid bet? He had still let her go as if she hadn't
meant anything to him. If he'd cared for her—*loved
her*—surely he would have fought for her? But no, he
had let her go without a fight, without a single word
of protest.

Had she really meant so little to him?

She schooled her features into a cold mask. 'So who was responsible for the bet?'

He looked away, a frown pulling heavily at his brow. 'It was a mate of mine called Tom.' He paused for a moment as if he found the disclosure painful. 'He always was a bit of a pot stirrer.'

Something about his tone made her ask, 'Was?'

His expression was as bleak as his voice. 'He was killed in a skiing accident six weeks after we broke up.'

Isabelle captured her lip between her teeth for a moment. She understood grief all too well. The initial shock of it, and then the stabbing ache of it that caught one off guard even years on. 'I'm sorry.'

He accepted her condolences with an on-off smile that didn't make the distance to his eyes. 'I hope he forgives me for ratting on him.'

Isabelle frowned. 'You weren't ever going to tell me?'

He lifted a shoulder in a shrugging movement. 'I didn't figure we'd cross paths again.'

And that didn't bother you one little bit, did it? The words hovered on the end of her tongue. She longed to throw them in his face but to do so would be to reveal her heartbreak over the termination of their relationship. It was easier to let him think she agreed with him. What did she have to gain by revealing how much power he'd had over her back then?

Instead she chewed at her lower lip as she got her head around his revelation. She had fuelled her hatred of him with the issue of the bet well before she found out about her pregnancy. It was the one thing that had stuck in her craw—that he had used her in such a despicable way. It had hardened her heart until it was a block of marble inside her chest. It had made her bitter and resentful towards him. It had made her determined to resist any other man's attempt to get close to her. She had cordoned herself off emotionally. She had spent the past decade proving to herself that she didn't need intimacy—from anyone.

To suddenly find her anger had hit the wrong target was...destabilising. It made her feel the high moral ground she had been standing on all this time was now shifting beneath her feet.

Spencer came back to where she was standing. His expression was grave with concern as he met her gaze. 'Tell me you don't drink yourself into a stupor every night because of me.'

Isabelle laughed off the suggestion. 'You would've had to have meant far more to me than a fling to have me resort to that.'

He took her chin between his finger and thumb, preventing her gaze from skittering away from his. She held her breath as his eyes went back and forth between hers. Searching. Penetrating. Uncovering. 'You've never had a serious relationship,' he said.

'Is that a question or a supposition?'

He studied her for another couple of beats. 'Most women your age are looking for the fairy tale. Why not you?'

Isabelle kept her mask in place. 'I'm a career girl, that's why. The hotel is my focus. I haven't got time for anything else.'

'And that fulfils you?'

'Why wouldn't it?' she said, and pointedly removed his hand from her chin. 'Your career fulfils you, doesn't it?'

Something moved across his expression like a ripple

over the surface of a lake. But then he covered it with a wry twist of his lips. 'Touché.'

Isabelle moved back out of his contact zone. Her body had an annoying habit of being drawn to him like a magnet draws metal. His touch lit fires beneath her skin. She could feel the nerves twitching and leaping as if in search of more of his drugging caresses. 'I love my job.' She said it with as much conviction as she could muster. 'I've aspired to run this place since I was a child. I hate it when people—men, mostly—assume I'm not one hundred per cent committed to my career.'

'You don't want a family one day?'

She kept her body language neutral. 'Do you?'

That flicker went across his face again before he masked it. 'I've thought about it but I'm not sure I'm cut out for it. It's a lot of responsibility to take on.'

'You're not close to your father?'

A muscle ticked at the corner of his mouth. 'No,' he said. 'But then, I'm not close to either of my parents.'

'At least you still have both of them.'

There was an echoing silence.

Isabelle wished she hadn't disclosed her inner loneliness—the adult orphan with no one to watch out for her. The burden of responsibility she carried because there was no parent figure to share it with. What was it about Spencer tonight that made her want to unburden herself? She wasn't one for sharing confidences. She kept things to herself, because she firmly agreed with the adage of less said soonest mended. She wasn't the type of girl to lean on a man, especially as the men in her life had always let her down. Her father, her brother and, of course, Spencer himself.

He glanced at the sofa where Atticus was looking

at him with an unblinking stare. 'About the cat...' He turned back but paused as if working his way to a decision inside his head.

'You're not going to make me get rid of him, are you.' Isabelle framed it as a statement rather than a question in the hope she wouldn't sound as if she were pleading.

A frown tugged at his brow once more. 'Wouldn't it be better for him and you to live outside the hotel?'

She straightened her shoulders. 'This is my home.'

'You don't want more than...this?' He waved his hand to encompass their surroundings.

She kept her expression blank. 'What else could I want?'

His eyes studied hers for a beat or two before shifting away. But this time she got the feeling he was not so much trying to search for something in hers but to keep something hidden in his.

She watched as he moved to the door, his hand pausing on the doorknob for a moment before he turned it and left without even saying goodnight.

CHAPTER SIX

SPENCER LOOKED SIGHTLESSLY at the vista of New York City from his hotel suite windows. For all the glitz and flash and sparkle on show he could have been looking at a windswept desert. Isabelle's revelation about her innocence had shocked him to the core.

Had he really been *that* insensitive back then? What sort of man had he been to miss something as significant as that?

His skin crawled with disgust and self-loathing. He'd been so intent on his mission to seduce the ice-cool socialite he hadn't realised she was a virgin. It was a picture of himself he didn't like. Couldn't bear to examine. How could he have been so fixated on the challenge of bedding her he hadn't sensed her inexperience?

What sort of man did that make him?

He thought back to their first time. His gut clenched with guilt—*her* first time. Surely if he'd hurt her he would have noticed? It worried him, sickened him, to think he might have missed it out of sheer arrogance.

He'd set his sights on her because she was different from his usual type, but he hadn't realised how different until now. It had never entered his head she was inexperienced. He put her earlier reluctance to get involved with him down to her reserved nature, her cool collectedness that was so attractive to him because he was used to women throwing themselves at him.

Isabelle had class and sophistication in spades. She held herself aloft, looking down at him as if he'd crawled out of a primeval swamp. Behind that cool elegant poise had hidden a passionate woman who responded to him with red-hot enthusiasm.

He had ruthlessly pursued her. Not stopping until he had her exactly where he wanted her. But one night hadn't been enough. Nor had two or even three. A week had gone past before he'd mentally taken stock. He didn't do relationships. He avoided the commitment and responsibility. He liked the freedom to move on when he wanted to without regrets or recriminations.

But with Isabelle he had broken every rule. He hadn't just seduced her. He'd dated her. Courted her. Showered her with gifts and taken her to places he had taken no other women. He'd enjoyed her company. He'd enjoyed her intelligence—that she could understand the world he lived in because she lived in it herself.

But what expectations had *she* brought to the relationship? She had only been two years younger than him but everyone knew women matured a whole lot earlier than men. Had she been looking for the fairy tale and envisaged him in it?

The thought sat uncomfortably with him. He wasn't into fairy tales. Not then and certainly not now. He wasn't even who she thought he was. He wasn't truly a Chatsfield. He was a fake. A fraud. An interloper who could be ousted at any moment. It hung over him like the sword of Damocles, the thought that if someone outside the family cottoned on he would be exposed.

Why hadn't she told him of her innocence? Or had she been keen to appear as sophisticated and street-wise as she acted?

Hammer blows of guilt pounded at his temples. He was not a cad. He was a playboy, sure, but not a man who didn't respect and honour women. He had never slept with a virgin, not even his first time had been with another virgin but someone three years older and with far more experience than him.

Up until Isabelle, sex had been sex, a physical need that could easily and conveniently be satisfied with a partner who wanted the same thing—a no-strings fling. He lived in the hook-up culture and made the most of it.

Was that why she hated him so vehemently? Because he hadn't lived up to her hopes of a happy-ever-after? Didn't all women cling to their first love? Imagining them to be The One. Had Isabelle seen him like that? As someone she could spend the rest of her life with?

There was a time when he had considered the pos-sibility of marrying and continuing the Chatsfield line, but overhearing his parents arguing that Christmas had ripped that plan to shreds. He wasn't part of the Chats-field line. The blood that flowed in his veins belonged to someone who had nothing whatsoever to do with hotels, other than to drink in them, a habit that in the end had cut short his life.

Spencer had thought Isabelle's hatred towards him was because of that ridiculous bet and more recently because of the hotel takeover. But to find she had another axe to grind against his guilt was lowering to say the least.

He had done some discreet research and found out she hadn't been in a serious relationship since her time with him...or none that anyone knew of. Didn't that say something? Had she been so invested in their relationship she had been devastated when it ended? She hadn't acted devastated. She'd acted angry. Coldly angry. And he had conveniently used her anger to get out of a relationship he hadn't known how to handle.

He wasn't used to needing people. He prided himself on his self-reliance, a self-reliance that had served him well once he found out about his biological origins. The thought of needing someone was anathema to him. Needing someone made you a bull's-eye target for disappointment.

Isabelle lived and breathed The Harrington. She worked long hours and lived on-site...with a contraband cat. That had truly gobsmacked him. She didn't present as the nurturing-a-pet type. She was aloof and standoffish in her dealings with people. Even her hand-picked staff were held at arm's length. But maybe a cat suited her. Cats were known to be aloof and haughty, a slave to no one.

There *were* health issues with having a cat in the hotel. He hadn't been making that up. But he could see why a single woman living in a hotel where she worked would want one. It was company of sorts. Someone to talk to when no one else would listen.

Sheesh, maybe he should get himself one.

Spencer moved away from the window with a ragged sigh. The muscles of his neck and shoulders felt like concrete. He had a headache behind his eyes that was

creeping dangerously close towards one of his migraines. His stomach was curdled with remorse. Shame.
Disgust at himself.

How could he have been so blind? What defect in
his personality—in his bastard lineage—had allowed
something like this to happen? What if he *had* hurt
her and she wasn't admitting it? He knew her to be
proud. Her uppity manner was one of the things he'd
found so attractive.

He was her first lover.

The thought kept coming back at him like the bars
of a song he couldn't get out of his head.

He hadn't taken things slowly that first time. He
hadn't made any allowances. He had been so driven
with lust they had come together in a firestorm of passion. The lead-up to their fling had been the longest and
yet most enjoyable foreplay of his life. She had resisted
his attempts to seduce her, which had only made him
all the more determined. When she finally capitulated
he had been triumphant.

The sex had been amazing. Not just because he'd
had to work for it harder than normal, but because
their bodies had a certain chemistry he hadn't felt before or with anyone else since. And not just that first
time, but every time. There was a level of intimacy between them. There was both passion and tenderness.
He remembered the way her fingertips would play up
and down his spine. He used to shiver with the delight
of her touch. She could bring him to his knees with
a single stroke of her fingers. She hadn't been coy in
pleasuring him. She had gone down on him with an
expertise he could only marvel at now he knew she
had been a novice. How had she known to touch him

like that? To read his body, to stroke him with her lips and tongue until his knees buckled and he exploded.

How was he going to handle this situation between himself and Isabelle now? The attraction was still there. On both sides. He felt it every time he was with her. She said she hated herself for it and no wonder. He was the enemy. He had acted with a scant disregard for her feelings. Feelings he had not sensed, not intuited, because he didn't deal in the currency of emotions. He was a facts-and-figures man. Feelings were something he ignored. Dismissed. Discounted. He wanted results and he went after them with a dogged determinism.

He was her first lover.

The sense of pride in that thought was probably leaning towards Neanderthal-like but he couldn't help it. He had been the first one to pleasure her, to bring her to orgasm with his body and his touch. He had been the first person to hold her in an intimate embrace that had shaken her body, creating shudders of ecstasy that he had felt reverberating through his own. He had been the first one to fill her with his length, to feel her body surround him, grip him, to contract against him in tight ripples of pleasure. How could he not feel some element of pride in being the first to share that with her? It made every other experience of sex he'd ever had seem almost tawdry in comparison.

Could he risk another fling/relationship with her? Would she accept it? She had offered herself to him in his office like a hooker. Cheapening herself as she accused him of cheapening her. He could so easily have taken her. His body had thrummed with need. Ached with it. Burned with it.

But he wasn't going to be manipulated by game

playing and point scoring. He liked to be the one in control of his affairs. If he got involved with her again there were things to weigh up. How would he juggle the complication of a relationship with his biggest work challenge of his career? Was that why she was offering herself to him? Knowing it would distract him from his goal? Why else would she want an affair with him? She hated him. And it seemed he had given her good reason for it.

But hate and lust were not uncommon bedfellows. Hating someone didn't mean you didn't want them like an addict wants a fix.

But how would the press see a relationship between him and Isabelle? As a marketing ploy it certainly had merit, but what did Isabelle want? What did she *really* want? She said she was a career woman. He got that. He understood not every woman wanted the domestic setup. But something about her made him think she wasn't being completely honest. In the past she had spoken briefly on the loss of her mother when she was seventeen. She hadn't gone into detail. He got the feeling she was relaying the information from some place outside of herself, as if the loss and grief had happened to another person and she was only reporting it. Her relationship with her father had become distant after his marriage to Liliana. But he had heard that from others, not her. He had heard nothing but praise for her from the hotel staff. They spoke of her dedication, her loyalty to them and to the hotel brand, the way she treated them as a family unit, all pulling together to achieve the best for the company. But for all that he could see she held herself at a professional distance. He noticed no one called her by her first name. Had she insisted on that or was that part of The Harrington ethos?

She kept so much of herself behind the screen of her poise and aloofness. Was it wrong to want to get closer to her, to get to know the woman behind the ice-maiden mask? Was it selfish to revisit what they had shared, to see if it was as unique and deeply satisfying as he remembered it?

When Isabelle turned up at her office the next morning there was a huge bunch of spring flowers on her desk.

'They're from Mr Chatsfield,' her secretary, Laura, said. 'He delivered them himself half an hour ago.'

Isabelle felt a blush crawl over her cheeks. In amongst the heady perfume of the flowers she could pick up a faint trace of Spencer's lemon and lime aftershave. It made her senses sing in spite of the pounding head-ache she was fighting off. 'Send a thank-you note to him,' she said.

Laura gave her a quizzical frown. 'You don't want to write it yourself?'

Isabelle kept her expression and her tone coolly in-different. 'No, why would I?'

Laura handed her the morning newspaper. 'Hmm… Maybe you shouldn't read this until you have some caffeine on board.'

She looked at the gossip section Laura had folded the paper open to. There was a photo of her and Spen-cer in the bar last night and a caption that said *Romance behind Chatsfield hotel merger?* Then the article below went a little further.

The David and Goliath battle between the giant Chatsfield hotel chain and the stately Harrington has come to a truce…or should we say tryst?

Sworn enemies Englishman Spencer Chats-field and New Yorker Isabelle Harrington were seen leaving The Harrington hotel bar together late last night. Our source hinted there is more behind the Chatsfield takeover of The Harrington than meets the eye.

Has Miss Harrington's earlier resistance to the takeover been a cover-up for a clandestine affair with the now-major shareholder, Spencer Chatsfield?

Isabelle shoved the paper to one side before she could read any more. 'You're right. I need some caffeine.'

Laura let out a wistful sigh. 'If I were forty years younger I'd make a play for him myself.'

Laura had been at The Harrington for as long as Isabelle could remember. Whenever she used to come into her father's office, Laura would sneak her a couple of pieces of candy from her supply in the drawer of her desk. Isabelle knew she should have replaced her with someone a lot younger and a lot less interested in her private life but she hadn't been able to bring herself to do it. Yet.

She gave her a speaking look. 'Don't you have work to do?'

Laura was undaunted. But then it was probably hard to be daunted by someone you had seen go from bobby socks to braces and budding breasts and puppy fat to adulthood. 'I think it's unfair how your stepmother handed Spencer Chatsfield those shares. You're the one who's done all the hard work around here. I'd hate to see the hotel lose its special charm. It's not that The

Chatsfields aren't great hotels or anything. And I'm sure Mr Chatsfield is a very nice person and all. But they're not The Harrington, are they?'

Isabelle let out a short breath. 'No.'

Laura picked up the newspaper off Isabelle's desk and examined the photo. 'He's very good-looking, isn't he? Gorgeous blue eyes.'

'Have you sent those outstanding accounts I asked you to send yesterday?'

'And his accent is so posh,' Laura said. 'I could listen to him read the phone directory. I wonder if he went to Eton like Prince William and Prince Harry?'

Isabelle pressed two of her fingers to the left side of her temple where a pneumatic drill seemed to be boring into her skull. 'Forget about the coffee. I'll have tea instead. Black, no sugar.'

Laura lifted her brows so high they disappeared beneath the neatly trimmed bangs of her steel-grey bob. 'But you never drink tea.'

'Once you've done that, I don't want to be disturbed.'

'What if it's Mr Chatsfield?'

'*Especially* if it's Mr Chatsfield.'

Laura frowned again. 'But he's your boss now, isn't he? You can't order him about as if he's one of the junior staff.'

Isabelle ground her teeth and then wished she hadn't as it caused another fissure in the plates of her skull. 'He's also your boss so you'd better keep on your toes. He might want someone fresh out of nursery school instead of someone nudging retirement.'

'I really like him,' Laura said. 'I know that sounds a bit disloyal and all. I expected him to be stuck-up but he spoke to me as if I was really integral to the hotel. Mind you, I've been here long enough to know a few things about the business.' She chuckled. 'The stories I could tell him. I could write a book.'

'Every staff member is integral to The Harrington,' Isabelle said as if she were reading it from the mission statement.

Laura tucked the newspaper under her arm. 'I'll get your tea.'

Isabelle leaned her elbows on the desk and cradled her aching head in her hands. She hadn't thought about what the press would make of her and Spencer being seen together. Well, she had but preferred *not* to think about it. Spencer was in and out of the papers all the time. He and his cousins kept readers entertained with their supposed exploits. If they did even half of what the press documented they would never get a wink of sleep or do a day's work.

She, on the other hand, did her best to steer clear of gossip and innuendo. It was undignified. She didn't want to tarnish the hotel's brand with anything unseemly, even if it was entirely fabricated, which most of the sensationalised gossip pieces were. The very small private life she had was conducted out of the glare of the spotlight and she intended to keep it that way.

The door of her office opened and she didn't bother looking up. 'Just leave it on the desk.'

'Hangover?' Spencer said.

Isabelle lifted her head so quickly she saw a school of silverfish float past her eyes. She blinked them away and averted her gaze from his. 'If you haven't got hot tea or paracetamol with you, then don't come any closer.'

'How about an apology?'

She chanced a quick glance at him. 'Thanks for the flowers,' she said. 'I was going to send a note...'

'Yes, so your secretary said.'

She dropped her gaze and began to chew at the corner of her mouth. 'I suppose she showed you the paper?'

'She's very efficient, isn't she?'

Isabelle looked at him again. He looked disgustingly fresh and vital. Clean-shaven, clear-eyed and well-rested. He clearly hadn't been up half the night restless with unspent sexual energy. Or maybe he'd called in someone to fix that little problem for him. The thought made her stomach clench. 'Did you see anyone taking a picture of us last night?'

'No, but do you know how many smartphones are in any one place at any one time?' he said. 'Everyone's a celebrity snapper these days.'

She pushed back from the desk and winced as her head protested. 'I don't like being talked about. My private life is my business, no one else's.'

'Do you even have one?'

Isabelle raised her chin. 'Like I said, it's my business.'

His eyes studied hers for a lengthy moment. 'Did you read my card?'

'What card?'

He unpinned it from the arrangement of flowers and handed it to her. Her stomach flipped over when his fingers brushed hers. She slipped the card out of the tiny envelope and looked at the dark scrawl of his handwritten note. *I'm sorry. S.*

Isabelle poked the card back inside the envelope and

gave him an arch look. 'Does that mean you're going to hand me the two per cent shares?'

A frown pulled hard at his forehead. 'No, it does not.'

She handed him the card. 'You can keep your apology.'

He ignored the outstretched card. 'Damn it, Isabelle,' he said. 'If I'd known I would've—'

'What?' she said in a mocking tone. 'Been gentle with me?'

A dull flush rode over his aristocratic cheekbones. 'If I hurt you, then I'm deeply sorry.'

She folded her arms across her body and shot him a fiery glare. 'You hurt me more by all but stealing my hotel off me.'

He tightened his mouth until it was almost flat. 'I didn't force your stepmother to hand those shares over. You heard what she said. She thought it was the best thing to do under the circumstances.'

Isabelle flung her arms out in scorn. 'Oh, yes, how could I forget? Liliana knows the best thing to do for me *under the circumstances*. What a load of crock. She doesn't *know* me. She doesn't understand anything about me because if she did she would never have given you those shares.'

'Did she know we were once involved?'

'No.'

'Did you tell anyone about us?'

Isabelle gave him a hard look. 'I certainly didn't give a tell-all interview to the press the first chance I got.'

His brows came together again. 'You think *I'm* responsible for what's in this morning's paper?'

'Aren't you?'

'No.'

There was a knock at the door and Laura came bustling in with tea for two on a tray. She gave Isabelle a beaming smile as she set the tray down on the desk. 'I figured you and Mr Chatsfield would have heaps to chat about. I brought cookies too.'

'Thank you,' Isabelle said stiffly.

'Thanks, Laura,' Spencer said with a smile. 'Chocolate chip are my favourite.'

Laura walked out backwards as if she couldn't bear to drag her gaze away from Spencer's tall handsome frame. Once the door was closed Isabelle turned to him with an arch of her brows. 'Another conquest?'

'How long's she been here?'

'I inherited her. She was my father's secretary. She's excellent at her job. She knows the business inside and out.' Isabelle knew she sounded like she was rationalising Laura's continued employment but she was dreading the time when she would have to let the older woman go. Laura understood her need to hold on to The Harrington. She understood it was the only family Isabelle could identify with now. The loss of her mother, and then her father's remarriage and then his death, Jonathan's irresponsibility and her sisters' lives outside the hotel business meant the hotel was the only constant she could cling to. It was her anchor, the only place where things could be controlled and timetabled.

'You sound like you're really fond of her.'

Isabelle shrugged one shoulder. 'I'm running a business, not a friendship society. I'd fire her tomorrow if she wasn't doing her job.'

He gave a tilted smile. 'Liar.'

She pulled out her chair and made a point of positioning it just so behind her desk as she sat down. She tossed her hair back with a little roll of her neck and shoulders and faced him squarely. 'What did you want to see me about? I have work to do so if you could make it snappy...'

'I've been thinking about our situation.'

She glared at him across the desk. 'There is no situation apart from you being a ruthless player who takes anything that piques his fancy without considering how other people feel about it.'

There was a moment of tense silence.

'Fine. I probably deserved that.' He let out a long sigh. 'I admit that when I met you in London I did everything I could to seduce you. I saw you as a challenge I couldn't—wouldn't—resist. I didn't have the sensitivity back then to realise you were playing hard to get because you were waiting for Mr Right.'

'I wasn't waiting for Mr Anybody,' Isabelle said. 'I just hadn't got around to having sex. I was too busy holding this place together and watching out for my younger sisters.' She got up from behind her desk and busied herself pouring tea. 'Do you still have it with milk and half a sugar?'

'How on earth did you remember that?'

Isabelle slipped her gaze out of reach of his. 'I seem to remember we drank a lot of tea back then.' She handed him a cup but was dismayed at the way her hand was shaking, making the cup rattle in its saucer.

He took the cup from her and put it down on the desk before he came around to her side of the desk and took her hands in his and brought her to her feet in front of him. His eyes meshed with hers in a searching look that made her heart contract. His thumbs stroked over the backs of her hands, smoothing, soothing strokes that made her legs feel tingly from the tops of her thighs to the backs of her knees. 'It doesn't have to be this way between us, Isabelle.'

She swallowed a sudden lump in her throat. He had an unnerving skill at disarming her when she least expected it. His gentle voice, tender touch and focused gaze made her defences crumble. Why couldn't he stick with his smart-ass comments and teasing smiles? Why did he have to go all sweet and sensitive on her? It wasn't fair. 'What do you mean?'

His eyes drifted to her mouth, watched as the tip of her tongue sneaked out to moisten it. 'Enemies. Rivals. Fighting all the time.'

Something low and deep in her belly wobbled. 'What are you suggesting?'

His eyes came back to hers. Dark. Deep. Unfathomable. 'We could do what the paper thinks we're already doing.'

Isabelle wondered what his motivation was. She could see the benefits businesswise. It wouldn't look good for the Chatsfield brand to be seen as a ruthless giant overtaking a small family-run hotel. If the takeover were seen as a more personal interest on his part, cooperative rather than a conquest, it would benefit both parties. 'Have an affair, you mean?'

'Neither of us is married so it wouldn't be an affair.'

'What would it be?'

'A relationship.'

She looked at his chin as she caught her breath. *A relationship?* With the man who didn't *do* relationships? Her heart began to hammer. Her body began to stir in excitement. Could she do it? Could she have a relationship with him and settle the ache of her flesh once and for all?

She could keep control this time. She wouldn't get too ahead of herself. There would be no foolish thinking of living happily ever after. No thinking of cute little babies and making a family together. No falling in love and expecting to be loved in turn.

It would be about sex and sex only. She would indulge in a lust fest and get out before he could end it. It would settle the score between them. Leave her with a sense of justice. If she couldn't get the shares back, then at least she would have her pride.

Isabelle kept her expression nonchalant as she met his gaze once more. 'Do you have a specific timeline in mind?'

His eyes moved between each of hers in a back and forth motion that was both mesmerising and dangerous. She had to fight hard to keep her emotions veiled. He might have missed her innocence in the past but it was clear he wasn't going to miss a trick now. There was an intensity to his gaze, a sharply observant quality that made her feel as if he could see into her soul. 'Why don't we take it a day at a time?' he said.

Isabelle chastised herself for her sense of disappointment. What had she been expecting him to say? That he wanted her to be with him for ever? He would never say that. Not to her. Not to anyone. 'I have a couple of stipulations,' she said.

Nothing showed on his expression. Not a muscle moved. It was almost too controlled. He didn't even blink. 'Which are?'

'No staying overnight.'

He acknowledged that with a slight movement of his mouth. Not quite a smile. Not quite a grimace. 'Fine,' he said. 'What else?'

'No gifts.'

He glanced at the flowers on her desk. 'You want me to get rid of them?'

'No. I don't want to have to explain their absence to Laura.'

This time he did smile but it was one part humour, three parts derision. 'Anything else?'

Isabelle squared her shoulders. Steeled her resolve. 'No kissing.'

His eyebrows lifted a fraction. 'That's a biggie.'

'It's not negotiable.'

He studied her for a long throbbing moment.

Isabelle got the feeling he was revisiting every one of their kisses. Her own mind filled with images of their mouths locked together in passionate exchanges, his tongue tangling with hers, duelling, subduing, conquering.

She couldn't quite control the impulse to glance at his mouth. He was freshly shaven but even so she could see the pinpricks of stubble on his lean jaw and around the sculpted perfection of his mouth. She could smell the light citrus tang of his aftershave. It teased her nostrils, wafting over her in a subtle but powerfully evocative manner. It was far more alluring than the fragrant bouquet of flowers sitting on her desk. She remembered the intimate scent of him, the musk and male scent that had delighted her senses. Drugged and stoned her into sensual overload.

His gaze became sleepily hooded as he looked at her mouth. Was he remembering the times she had pleasured him? She had gone on instinct alone, using her lips and tongue to push him to the brink. Teasing him, tasting the essence of him, feeling the power of him and the vulnerability. He had done the same to her; subjecting her to mind-blowing orgasms, making her thrash and writhe as the spasms moved through her body like oversize waves.

The erotic memories were like another presence in the room. They charged the air with a fizzing static that made the flesh on Isabelle's arms lift in a shower of goose bumps. She could feel her inner core contracting. Remembering. Wanting. Aching.

She became aware of her breasts inside the lace cup of her bra. They pushed against the cobweb of fabric, reminding her of their need to feel his lips and tongue, the sexy scrape of his teeth, the suck and draw of his mouth.

A glint came into his eyes as they reconnected with hers. 'How about I strike a little deal with you?'

She shook her head. 'Na-ah. No deals.'

'You should listen to what's on the table before you reject it out of hand,' he said. 'Sound business practice. Otherwise who knows? You might be missing out on the deal of a lifetime.'

What would he put on the line? Isabelle wondered. Liliana's shares? Surely not...*would he*? A shiver scooted down her spine and shot back up again, making the hairs on the back of her neck tingle at the roots. 'Go on.'

He held her gaze in a heart-stopping lock. 'If either of us breaks the kissing rule we have to forfeit something.'

Another frisson of excitement coursed through her. 'Two per cent?'

One of his brows lifted. 'You'd risk that much?'

She frowned as disappointment collided with elation. 'What were you going to suggest?'

'One per cent.'

Isabelle chewed it over for a moment. If he won he'd be even further in front with fifty-two per cent. But if *she* won she would be level with him at fifty per cent. At least then she would be equal shareholder.

But if she lost...

Her stomach pitched at the thought. Was that why he'd offered the deal? He wanted more than he already had. He was a businessman first and foremost. He wouldn't let a 'relationship' get in the way of a business deal. She would be foolish to think he was trying to balance things out of consideration for her. The flowers were a nice touch, but she was not so easily wooed this time around. She had laid down the rules. He was trying to bend them to serve his interests.

She *wouldn't* lose. She would not allow herself to lose. This was her chance to claw back what should have been hers in the first place.

'Okay,' she said. 'You're on.'

His mouth kicked up at one corner. 'You're so confident you're going to win.'

Isabelle gave him a self-assured smile. 'But of course.'

She watched as his gaze went back to her mouth and back to her eyes, measuring, calculating. 'What if *you* lose?' he said.

'I won't.' Her voice sounded far more confident than she felt. She knew him well enough to know he would test her at every corner. He would tease and tempt her until she cracked. But with the shares as her incentive she was going to fight with every cell in her body to win. It was her chance to show him what she was made of. Not soppy warm emotion and vulnerability, but cold, hard steel.

He held out his hand. 'Shall we shake on it?'

Isabelle slipped her hand into the warm cage of his, her stomach doing a somersault as his fingers closed around hers. The heat passing from his body to hers lit spot fires in her flesh: along each of her fingers, from her wrist and up her arms, over her shoulder and down the length of her spine to the secret cave of her womanhood. Never had a handshake felt more intimate. It was like he was caressing her with his mind, stirring her into a molten pool of longing.

She gave herself a mental slap and pulled her hand away. 'Um, shouldn't we have something legal drawn up?'

His blue eyes smouldered as they held hers. 'You don't trust a gentleman's agreement?'

Isabelle gave him an arch look. 'You said you weren't a gentleman, remember?'

CHAPTER SEVEN

IF ONLY SHE KNEW, Spencer thought. 'What are you doing for lunch?' he said.

She blinked as if she found the swift subject change disorienting. 'Nothing…I usually have something at my desk.'

'Why don't we have a working lunch in my office?' he said. 'I'll get the kitchen to send up a tray.'

She gave him a guarded look. 'Why can't we go out or have it in the restaurant downstairs?'

Spencer knew what she was doing. She was trying to keep from being alone with him. He smiled to himself. He'd only agreed to her rules because he knew she needed time to get her head around being involved with him again. He hadn't handled things well in the past but that wasn't to say he couldn't make up some ground. He found her company so stimulating. She was feisty and spirited, passionate and yet determined not to show it. 'I thought you might find the press a bit intrusive,' he said. 'They'll be out in packs looking for a confirmation about our relationship.'

She chewed at her lower lip, pulling it almost the whole way into her mouth before releasing it. 'Fine. Your office it is. What time?'

He watched as the blood returned to her lips in a pink tide. His lips tingled at the memory of how those full soft lips felt against his own. She had a bee-stung curve to her mouth, a lush youthful bow that never failed to draw his gaze. 'Shall we say one?'

'Fine.' She gave a brisk nod and marched back behind her desk. He got the feeling she was using it as a barricade. She stood behind it with her hands braced on the back of her office chair. 'Will that be all?'

He searched her gaze for any trace of the girl he had met in London, the girl whose smile had tugged on something in his chest. Was he crazy to play such a dangerous game with her? He liked risks but only the ones he could count on cashing in.

She wasn't that guileless girl with the shy smile anyanmore. She was a cool-headed businesswoman who had an agenda—a goal she put before everything. She wanted major share of The Harrington and was prepared to fight hard and dirty for it.

He was confident he had her covered. How hard could it be? She had set up her silly little rules, which amused him more than anything. How long would she keep up the no-kissing thing? Her mouth was made for kissing. Never had he been with a woman who could kiss with as much enthusiasm and passion as she did.

But there were other ways to kiss. He remembered how her breasts had felt against his lips and tongue. The silky feel of her skin, the smooth satin of it as his stubble grazed it, often times leaving a mark. The thought of his body branding her as his triggered something deeply primal in him.

Then there was her neck, the creamy swan-like

length of it, and her hands with their dainty, soft fingertips that could stir such a storm in his blood.

And yet, there was a hardened quality to her now that made him wonder if he had underestimated her. He needed time with her. Uninterrupted time where he could explore the chemistry that fizzed like a current between them, the chemistry she was all too aware of and clearly trying to control on her terms. What was she frightened of? They were both fully mature adults who had a desire for each other that had never quite gone away. She insisted she was a career girl, that marriage and family were not a driving passion for her. He had said much the same, which made them equals in what they wanted out of their relationship.

How can you be equals when you own majority share?

The little voice was like a tap on Spencer's shoulder. A reminder that nothing was equal between him and Isabelle while he was her boss. He was in charge of her hotel. The hotel she had poured years of her life into. He had been appointed major shareholder by a stroke of luck rather than anything he had worked for. The victory should taste sweeter than it did. He had strived hard for this opportunity to prove himself to his family, but in doing so he had to negotiate a way to manage Isabelle and their past history. It went against everything he had worked for to simply hand over the shares in a goodwill gesture. What if in a fit of revenge she sold them to a competitor? He didn't know enough about her motives to trust her. She had expressed her anger at him from day one. The lust that pulsed between them didn't cancel out her fury, if anything he thought it fuelled it. She resented the fact she wanted him. She hated herself for it. She saw it as a weakness in herself while he delighted in it. He had agreed to her little rules with their one per cent stake because he knew he could win. He was sure of it.

'I've changed my mind about lunch,' he said. 'Let's make it dinner.'

Her eyelids flickered. 'Dinner?'

'In my suite.'

Her throat rose and fell over a swallow, her cheeks flushing a faint rosy pink. 'If you wish.'

He ran his gaze over her neat and trim knee-length dress with its schoolmarmish jacket. Had she dressed so primly to keep her body from betraying her? The tailored clothes kept the swell of her curves contained; there was no hint of cleavage or bare arms and shoulders. She was buttoned up but he could feel the passion that simmered beneath the surface. It was an electric energy in her, an energy that collided with his every time their gazes met. 'Wear something comfortable.'

Her whisky-brown eyes flashed at him with a hint of defiance. 'I'll wear what I damn well want.'

He raised his hand to his lips and kissed the end of his index and middle finger and then blew it across to her with a devilish wink. 'See you at seven.'

Isabelle let out a long furious breath as the door closed behind him. Her skin was hot. Her nerves were jangled. Her body was quivering with traitorous anticipation and need. Was she making the biggest mistake—the second biggest mistake—of her life by playing such a dangerous game with him?

But it would be worth it if she could claw back even one per cent of those shares.

He wanted her.

That was his weakness, the only one she could see so far. He was a powerful enemy. Powerful and potent, so potent she could sense the testosterone oozing out of him every time he was in the same room as her. Which was why she had to keep him from kissing her. He could undo her with a single kiss. Kissing was too intimate, too emotional. She gave too much of herself when she kissed him. He drew it out of her like he had special powers. No one else could do it to her. No one else ever had. He had a magician's mouth, spellbinding, captivating. Unforgettable.

This way she would be able to control things, keep things on the level.

They would come together as equals this time. This was a business deal like any other. He wanted her. She wanted him. It was about sex, not emotion. She could do that. She could shut off her mind and let her body take over. She had done it before.

Laura gave a quick tap before popping her head around the door. 'Will I take the tea things now?'

'Sure.'

She loaded the things on the tray before looking at Isabelle with her mother-hen look. 'Everything all right?'

She forced a tight smile. 'Of course.'

Laura pursed her lips thoughtfully for a moment. 'You know, you wouldn't be human if you didn't fancy him a teensy weensy bit. A man as good-looking as that would set any girl's heart aflutter.'

Isabelle felt her cheeks ripen with betraying colour. 'Looks aren't everything.'

Laura made a *phfft* sound. 'You've got a lot in common both coming from hotel families and you're not getting any younger. I was married and had three children by the time I was your age.'

Isabelle gave her a stony look. 'I'm a career woman. How many times do I have to say it? Not every woman wants the white picket fence, you know.'

Laura shifted her lips from side to side. 'Your mom would've loved to see you settled with a nice man. Not someone like your father—begging your pardon for speaking out of turn—but he wasn't Father of the Year material even if he was a damn good boss way back in the day when he was still interested in this place. No, you need a man who'll stand up to you and for you. Someone who'll have your back no matter what.'

Isabelle mentally curled her top lip. 'I hardly think Spencer Chatsfield qualifies. He's a seasoned playboy.'

'Ah, but they make the best husbands,' Laura said. 'There's nothing better than a reformed rake. When they finally fall, they fall good and hard.'

Spencer falling in love? With her? What sort of a deluded fool would she be to dream of that scenario when it had so spectacularly failed in the past? If he was going to fall in love with her he would have done it when she was young and trusting and without a cynical and angry bone in her body. She was no longer that naive and accommodating girl. She was a driven workaholic with achievement and success on her mind, not love and happy-ever-after.

Isabelle pretended to be interested in the emails on her computer screen but it was all but impossible to ignore her secretary's hovering presence.

'There's a certain chemistry between you two, isn't there?' Laura said as she placed the sugar bowl on the tray. 'I felt it as soon as I came in before. The air was all but sizzling with it.'

'You're imagining it.'

'Am I?'

Isabelle met her gaze with a steely set to her features. 'I absolutely loathe the man.'

Laura's hazel eyes twinkled. 'Of course you do. It wouldn't be such great chemistry if you didn't.'

She shifted her gaze back to the computer screen. 'You're talking rubbish.'

'You hate him because he's got the upper hand,' Laura said. 'You've always been a competitive little thing. It's because you've had to fight to get noticed, being a girl and all. But not all men are like your father and your brother. Mr Chatsfield's got a certain quality. Yes, he's determined and a little ruthless but he respects you.'

Isabelle sat back in her chair with a cynical laugh. 'What on earth gives you that idea?'

Laura tilted her head towards the flower arrangement on her desk. 'Got to love a man who knows how to apologise.'

She jerked upright in her chair like a puppet pulled tightly on its strings. 'You read the card?'

''Course I did. I read all your mail unless it's marked private.'

Isabelle pressed her mouth flat. She didn't want to explain to Laura about her history with Spencer. The only person who knew the extent of it was her university friend Sophie. Not even her sisters knew.

But her secretary was no fool. How long before she figured it out for herself? How could Isabelle possibly hope to keep her relationship with him a secret if the staff saw her coming and going from his suite and him from hers? After what the press had already reported it would be difficult to pretend it was just to discuss business. Would it damage her reputation with the staff? Or would it enhance it? She knew she had a reputation for being cold and distant. Perhaps they would see her as more human if she indulged in a little fling with the new CEO.

'I'd prefer it in future if you would refrain from reading anything that comes from Spencer Chatsfield,' she said.

Laura's brows lifted. 'So it's true what the papers are saying? There is something going on between you two?'

Isabelle flicked her secretary an irritated glance. 'Since when has my private life been so important to you?'

'Since you got back from London all those years ago and froze everyone out,' Laura said. 'You changed. I noticed it the moment you got back. You stopped smiling. You wouldn't talk to anyone. You retreated into yourself like a snail does into its shell.'

Isabelle kept her expression neutral. 'It was a big change coming back to New York after being in London. I found it hard to fit back in.'

'I thought it was because of your father getting involved with Liliana and them marrying in such a rush, but it wasn't that, was it?'

Isabelle gripped the arms of her office chair. 'Haven't I given you enough work to do?'

Laura gave her a look over the top of her multifocal glasses. 'It was him, wasn't it? Mr Chatsfield was the one who broke your heart.'

Isabelle pushed up from her desk and wrapped her arms around her body. 'I don't want to talk about it.'

'It's been hard for you without a mother to lean on,' Laura said gently. 'You've had to be strong for Eleanore and Olivia while your brother always does what he darn well pleases. But isn't it time you took a little something for yourself? Had a bit of fun? Lived a little?'

Isabelle pushed out her lips on a whoosh of air. 'It's...complicated.'

'It always is when there's a man and a woman who want each other but feel they shouldn't,' Laura said. 'But what's the harm in having a little fling now you're older and wiser? Who knows? It might work out this time. What have you got to lose?'

Far more than you realise, Isabelle thought.

Isabelle placed one of her hands over her trembling belly as she stood outside Spencer's suite waiting for him to answer her knock. It was strange—*exciting* strange—to be going to his suite for the express purpose of having sex with him. It was so...clinical. Her old self would be appalled. Shocked. Ashamed even. But this wasn't about making love. This was about having sex. There was a difference and she had to keep reminding herself of it.

She heard the tread of footsteps and the door opened a crack but instead of Spencer hauling her into his arms as she expected he stood there with a frown knitting his brows. 'Can we do a rain check?' he said. 'Something's...erm...come up.'

For a horrible moment she wondered if he had someone else in the room. He was wearing a bathrobe and his hair was damp as if he had not long ago had a shower. Had he shared it with someone? Had he washed her back while she washed his? Who was it? The blonde from the other night? The thoughts flashed through her brain like missiles. It took every ounce of self-control not to peer past his broad shoulder. But then she realised his eyes were wincing against the light coming from the corridor and his face was unusually pale, ashen beneath the light tan of his skin. 'Are you okay?' she asked.

'Forgive the cliché but I have a headache.'

Isabelle would've laughed at his dry humour except she knew enough about headaches to know what he was currently experiencing was a migraine. The light and sound sensitivity would be excruciating. 'Have you taken something for it?' she asked in a soft tone.

'Yeah, I have some prescription meds for it. They'll kick in soon. I was going to text you but I can barely see straight...' His words trailed off as he scraped a hand through his hair, wincing as if the touch was painful.

She touched him lightly on the arm. 'Here, let me help you to bed. You need to lie flat and keep the lights down.'

Surprisingly he allowed her to lead him to the bedroom. She drew back the covers and helped him out of his bathrobe so he could lie down. She couldn't stop herself from drinking in his toned frame and his masculine form. Even though he was far from arousal he still looked magnificent. Her body gave a little quiver of memory of how it had felt to have him plunging deep inside her.

To see him so weak and vulnerable, so ill and unlike his usual take-charge self, disarmed her determination to hate him. A wave of sympathy passed through her, making everything that was hard and tightly knotted in her loosen like an unwound ball of string. He was under a lot of pressure juggling the Chatsfield chain and now her hotel. Was his family putting pressure on him or was he doing it to himself?

Isabelle pulled herself up short. Why was she worrying about his stress levels? She was supposed to be keeping her emotions separate. He was the enemy. He had taken everything off her. So what if a little karma was making him suffer for it? It probably wasn't even a proper migraine. Either way he deserved it for making *her* stress levels go through the roof.

Isabelle carefully drew the sheets over him and turned the bedside lamp off. She saw him wince at the sound of the click of the switch. She went over to the windows and gently drew the curtains so the room was in darkness.

She stood in silence looking at him lying on the king-size bed. He hadn't removed the condom tower or the velvet ties, and the mirrors above and at the end of the bed were still in place. Even the mask was on the bedside table next to the pump pack of lubricant. The juxtaposition of her strategically placed orgy items with his helpless and vulnerable body suddenly made her feel ashamed.

She tiptoed out of the bedroom and softly closed the door.

CHAPTER EIGHT

SPENCER WOKE FROM a deep sleep to find his head was still fuzzy from the migraine medication but the pain had lessened to a mild ache behind his eyes. He gingerly swung his legs over the edge of the bed, testing his balance and nausea level. He rose from the bed and used the bathroom, grimacing at his reflection in the mirror. He'd been experiencing migraines since he was twenty-nine. No surprise. The shock of finding out he wasn't his father's son had left him with a tendency for tension headaches that could quickly turn into a debilitating migraine. They occurred less frequently than they had, but they were still frequent enough to cause him a great deal of inconvenience.

Like last night's date with Isabelle.

He dragged a hand down his unshaven face, the sound of his stubble against his skin loud in the silence of the suite. He'd been so racked with pain and meds he couldn't recall much other than that she had helped him get into bed. It was humiliating to have her see him so prostrate. He never let anyone see him like that. Normally he did what he had to do—locked himself away until the migraine passed. But somehow her turning up before he could cancel their date had caught him off guard.

Spencer washed his face and brushed his teeth to get rid of the stale gym-sock feel in his mouth before coming out to the sitting room of the suite. He stopped short when he saw a small figure curled up on one of the sofas. Isabelle was sleeping with her cheek resting on one of her hands, her legs curled up like a child's, a scatter cushion cuddled close to her chest as if she had sought its comfort during the night.

He stood there watching the rise and fall of her chest as she breathed. She was still dressed in the little black dress and a three-quarter-length-sleeve cardigan she had been wearing last night. There was a single strand of pearls around her neck and pearl studs in her ears. She was wearing makeup, not too much, not too little—just enough to highlight the aristocratic shape of her cheekbones and enhance the shape and depth of her eyes.

The classiness of her never failed to amaze him. She had ostensibly been coming to have sex with him and yet she had dressed as if she were coming to a formal meeting.

He crossed the floor on silent footsteps and stood looking down at her for a long moment. She was so beautiful when she wasn't trying to gouge his eyes out. Before he was even aware he was doing it he gently brushed back a strand or two of her hair that had come loose from the neat chignon at the back of her head.

Her eyes suddenly sprang open and she jerked upright. 'Oh! I must've fallen asleep.' Her cheeks bloomed with colour as she saw he was wearing nothing but a towel hitched around his hips. 'How are you, um, feeling?'

He smiled as her eyes stayed fixedly on his as if she wasn't game enough to lower it to where his body was already stirring. 'Fighting fit.'

She rose from the sofa and straightened her crumpled dress, her gaze slipping out of the reach of his. 'I'd better let you get ready for work...'

'Wait.' He put a hand on her arm, turning her to look at him. 'What's the hurry? It's early still.'

Her brown eyes were smudged underneath where her makeup had run. It gave her an adorable panda look that was at odds with her usual well-put-together composure. Her small even white teeth sank into the soft pillow of her lips and his groin tightened with the urge to feel those beautiful lips on his, to feel the scrape of those teeth against his mouth in a playful bite.

He pressed the pad of his thumb against her lower lip, brushing it across the width of it, watching as the blood ebbed and flowed. He heard her catch her breath, the swift little uptake of air reminding him of the first time he had kissed her. The way she had gasped in surprise as his mouth had met hers, the way her lips had felt like velvet beneath his. The sweet vanilla taste of her and the shy dart of her tongue as he called it into play with his.

No kissing, remember?

Why did he feel like he would die if he didn't kiss her right now?

He bent his head so he could lower his mouth to the side of her neck just below her earlobe. He felt her shiver against him, her whole body quaking as his lips touched the sensitive skin. She smelt of gardenia or was it lily of the valley? A rich fragrance, redolent of times gone past. 'Am I allowed to kiss you here?' he said against her skin stretched over her collarbone.

She shivered again, her body leaning into him as if pulled by a magnetic force. 'Y-yes...' The word was a whisper of sound, soft, breathless.

He moved his mouth to her earlobe, flicking it lightly with the tip of his tongue. 'How about here?'

'Yes...' Her voice came out like a croak. *'Yes...'*

He took her earlobe between his teeth in a gentle nip, just enough pressure to keep her tethered to him. She shuddered against him, a soft groan escaping from her lips. He brought his mouth down the side of her neck, pausing along the way to nibble at her softly scented skin, listening to every intake of breath, feeling every delighted shudder pass through her body, making his own body taut with burning, raging desire.

He slipped her cardigan off her shoulders and slowly undid the zipper at the back of her dress, exposing the cap of her shoulder so he could press his lips to it, to swirl his tongue over it as she made little mewling sounds that incited his lust all the more. He could feel his erection tenting the towel that covered him, the pressure of want building at a frantic pace.

As if she read his mind or his body or both she put her hands to the knot on his towel and it slipped to the floor. The feel of her cool small hand around him almost sent him over the edge. He reined in the urge and concentrated on getting her naked.

Her dress joined his towel on the floor while he unfastened her bra. He bent his mouth to the upper curve of her right breast, gliding his lips over the smooth, creamy flesh, staying clear of her budded nipple until she begged him to take it by pressing closer with a soft little needy moan. He circled it with his tongue, and then gently suckled it with his mouth, doing the same to the left breast while she tilted her head sideways, her soft little cries of pleasure making his self-control strain at the leash.

His hands went to the pair of knickers she was wearing, a scrap of lace that was already damp. He slid them down past her thighs and she stepped out of them, leaning her hands on his shoulders for balance.

He stroked her entrance with his middle finger, a light barely-there touch that evoked another whole body shudder from her. He slid his finger into her, the tight and rippling grip of her body sending his senses into a tailspin of anticipation.

She pressed against his touch, searching for more friction. He tantalised her with rhythmic strokes, feeling the swell of her clitoris against his fingers. She writhed and gasped and then came apart in a shocked cry as if the sensations were a total surprise to her.

He held her by the waist, steadying her as she gathered herself, her cheeks and décolletage still flushed with the rosy tide of pleasure. Then, while holding his gaze in a smouldering lock, she went in search of him again, her fingers wrapping around his length, squeezing and stroking in turn. The pressure was perfect; she had an instinctive feel for his needs. She smeared his pre-ejaculate moisture over the swollen head of his penis, round and round in a tantalising circle that made his legs go weak at the knees. He knew what she was going to do by the look in her glinting brown eyes. The naughty-girl look made his backbone fizz as she went to her knees in front of him.

'Can I kiss you here?' she asked, her warm breath skating over his rigid flesh.

'You don't have to—' He cut off an expletive as she opened her mouth over him, the suction dizzyingly pleasurable.

With a mammoth effort of self-control he pulled back from her. 'Not without a condom.'

'But you used to let me...'

'It's safer with protection,' he said, leading her by the hand to the bedroom. 'Besides, we can't let all those you bought for me go to waste, can we?'

She gave him a sheepish look. 'I thought you said they were too small?'

He laughed as he took one from the nearest packet, handing it to her. 'Why don't you do a road test?'

Her fingers trembled as she sheathed him. He wasn't sure if it was shyness or lack of practice or heady excitement. She went to go down on him but he held her back. 'No. I want to be inside you.'

He walked her backwards to the bed, his thighs against hers, watching as her eyes sparkled with arousal. He joined her on the bed, coming down over her with his weight balanced on his arms. She opened her thighs for him, her arms looping around his neck, her eyes going to his mouth. He saw her catch her bottom lip between her teeth as if she only just remembered in time her no-kissing rule. He saw the glimmer of uncertainty or maybe it was regret in her gaze as it came back to his.

'Are you okay with this?' he asked.

'Sure.' She said it firmly, as if trying to convince herself rather than him. 'Why wouldn't I be? It's just sex.'

'So it is,' he said as he entered her with a long slow

thrust, his own breath catching as her body wrapped around him, swallowing him whole.

He began to move, building the pace so she wasn't rushed, but it took every bit of self-control he possessed to keep from coming. He told himself it was because he hadn't had a lover for a couple of months. He'd been busy with work and let his social/sex life slide. But he knew it was more to do with the chemistry between him and Isabelle, the fiery combustion of two strong wills that had resisted the pull of attraction up until now. The sheer force of it consumed him, making his thrusts harder, deeper, faster. He heard her gasping cries of encouragement, heard his own guttural groans—a sexy mingling of breathy moans that made him realise with a sharp pang how much he had missed her in the past decade.

He was so familiar with her body it felt like he had come home to a safe base, a place where he could let himself free knowing she was with him every step of the way. He slipped a hand between their rocking bodies, knowing just how much coaxing she needed to fly. It thrilled him to find her just as responsive to his touch as before. She gave a choked-off cry and came hard, contracting and pulsing around him until he tensed, paused and then flowed.

The sense of lassitude coursed through him like a warm tide, relaxing every muscle until he felt completely boneless. Her body was entangled with his, her breathing gradually slowing in soft little drifts against the side of his neck.

'I didn't rush you, did I?' he said into the silence.

She moved against him, her hands sliding down to

the base of his spine in a gentle caress that made his skin lift in a shiver. 'No. It was…you were…amazing.'

He eased onto his elbows to look at her, watching as her gaze drifted to his mouth as if pulled by a force she couldn't override. 'You were too. Better than I remembered.'

She looked at him briefly, then caught the edge of her lip in her teeth, and lowered her gaze back on his mouth. 'I would've thought you'd have forgotten given all the others since. A decade's a long time. You must've had hundreds of women. Thousands, maybe.'

He nudged up her chin to mesh his gaze with hers. 'The press exaggerate things. It's how they sell papers. If I did even half of what they said I'd be worn out by now.'

She gave him a sceptical look from beneath her lashes. 'So no one has stood out in all that time? No one special enough to keep longer than a few days?'

Spencer outlined her mouth with a lazy finger. 'I had a fortnight with a woman a couple of years back.'

Her brows moved together in a little frown. 'Who was it?'

'I can't remember her name.'

Her frown relaxed but didn't quite disappear. 'Did you end it or did she?'

'Me.'

'Why?'

He shrugged and rolled away, leaning over to dispose of the condom with a tissue from the box beside the bed. 'I got bored.'

When he turned back she was sitting upright with her arms hugging her bent knees close to her chest. Her dark hair was tousled, half up, half down, giving her a just-been-ravished look that made him harden all over again. 'What bores you about your lovers?' she asked.

He captured a loose strand of her hair and wound it around one of his fingers. 'Lots of things.'

'Such as?'

He unravelled her hair and tucked it behind her ear. 'Are you hungry?'

She frowned again. 'You didn't answer my question.'

Spencer swung his legs over the side of the bed. He didn't want to talk about his ex-lovers, especially not with her. He wasn't exactly proud of his track record with women. He knew his restlessness was his problem, not theirs. He had tried not to break any hearts and had always been clear about his intentions. No commitment. He saw sex as a physical need that needed to be attended to as required. Sometimes he used work to take his mind off the physical urge. Other times he indulged in mindless affairs to distract himself from the pressure of work. Sometimes—more times lately than he cared to admit—he'd abstained because it was easier than going through the routine of drink, dinner and mindless sex.

But making love with Isabelle reminded him of the way sex could be when two people were completely in tune with each other. The physical aspects were lifted to another level; one where there was not just a meeting of bodies but a connection that was like a harmony in a complicated melody. Pitch perfect, gorgeous cadences that made one's hairs lift on the back of the neck. He'd thought he'd imagined how good they were together, that he'd somehow got her confused with someone else.

Or rejigged his memory to make his time with her out to be something it wasn't.

But he hadn't been mistaken or misguided.

His body recognised hers, responded to hers with an intuitive sense that defied logic. Why was sex with her so satisfying? So exciting he wanted to have it again and again? He could feel the need building inside him, the tightening of his testicles, the flow of blood swelling him even as he fought to quell it.

He gripped the edge of the mattress, at war with himself. Should he push himself upright and get away from the temptation of her body or should he give in to the desire to lose himself in her, to indulge his senses until they were stoned with the intoxicating drug that was uniquely her?

As if she knew the war raging inside him she stroked a fingertip down the length of his spine to the crease at the top of his buttocks. He felt her press closer, her breasts brushing his shoulder blades in an erotic caress that made his senses go off like fireworks.

He turned and pushed her back on the bed, coming over her until his pelvis was flush with hers. His erection strained to get closer, to sink into her hot wet warmth and feel her contract around him. 'What time do you start work?' he asked.

'Seven, mostly.'

'That's early.'

She trailed her fingertip down the side of his jaw. 'Just as well we're not kissing as you'd give me beard rash with all that regrowth.'

He stilled her hand and turned it over and kissed the middle of her palm. 'You broke one of your rules.'

Her eyes flared. 'I did not!'

'You spent the night.'

'Not in your bed.'

'Same difference.'

She flashed him a look. 'No, it's not. You're twisting things.'

Spencer held her gaze for a beat. 'Why did you stay last night?'

Her eyes shifted to focus on his chin. 'I didn't intend to…I just waited until I was sure you were settled. I must have drifted off myself. It's a very comfortable sofa. But then all Harrington sofas are.' Her eyes came back to his with a prideful spark. 'I chose them specially. They're handmade. The fabrics are from Italy. Did you know that?'

He smiled at her attempt to rationalise her behaviour. 'You don't think it was a subconscious desire to spend the night with me in spite of your little rules?'

She flattened her mouth and pulled out of his hold. 'No, I do not.'

'Have a shower with me.'

'I have to feed Atticus and I need a change of clothes.'

He watched as she picked up her clothes with haughty dignity, her movement stiff and jerky. 'I want to see you tonight,' he said.

'I might be busy.'

He got off the bed and came over to where she was trying to zip up her dress. He turned her so her back was towards him and pulled the zip up. He swept the cloud of her hair to one side and pressed a kiss to the back of her neck. Her whole body shivered against him. He could sense the struggle in her to turn back around and offer herself to him. 'How about I come to your suite this time?' he said.

'You can't stay.'

He moved his mouth to the spot midway between her clavicle and her ear. 'I wouldn't dream of it.'

She tilted her head as he moved his mouth closer to her ear. A little gasp escaped from her mouth as his teeth took her earlobe in a soft little bite. Her bottom was pressed against his erection, tantalising him with the wicked thought of taking her from behind.

He ran his hands up from her hips to cup her breasts, shaping them, caressing them through her clothes. She made another sound of agonised pleasure and leaned further back against him. 'You don't play fair,' she said in a husky whisper.

He grazed the side of her neck with his stubble-surrounded mouth, his groin tightening painfully as the cheeks of her bottom pressed harder against him. 'Nor do you.'

She drew in a deep breath and stepped out of his hold, turning to face him with her colour high. 'I really have to go. I have a meeting with the housekeeping staff and there's the ball to organise and...'

He pressed a finger to her lips. 'Relax, darling. You never used to be such a stress bunny.'

She pulled his hand away from her face, flashing him a glittery look. 'I told you not to call me that.'

He hooked an eyebrow upwards. 'Another rule you want to assert?'

She compressed her lips. 'It doesn't matter how many rules I insist on, you'll find some way around them. It's what you do best. You're like the rest of your family.'

Spencer shook his head at her. 'Now that's where

you've got me all wrong. I'm nothing like my family. I don't even belong in it.'

Her forehead puckered in a puzzled frown. 'What do you mean?'

He let out a long slow breath, wondering if he was foolish for letting his guard down in front of her. But he was finding the stress of it exhausting. No wonder he was getting migraines. Pretending to be someone he wasn't ate away at him, gnawed at his conscience, and just lately it was chewing at his resolve to keep it a secret. Isabelle was a strange ally to be considering revealing all to but she had known him before and after. He had divided his life into those two categories— before he found out he was a bastard and after.

His life before had been one of privilege and wealth he had taken for granted like his younger brothers. After he found out he wasn't a Chatsfield his sense of entitlement dissipated. He suddenly realised how different his life would have been if he'd been brought up with his biological father. It might have been full of neglect and abuse, instead of unlimited wealth and luxury. Not that his childhood had been a happy one. How could it be with his mother treating him so distantly and his father even more so? It was only when he found out about his true paternity he'd understood why he had never felt at home. He still struggled with knowing where he belonged and whom he belonged to. Work was his only way of navigating his way through it. Proving himself worthy of the name he had no legal right to possess.

'Spencer?' Isabelle's soft voice found its way through the complicated maze of his thoughts. 'What do you mean you don't belong in your family?'

He looked at her uptilted face with her big brown eyes so wide and questioning. Her soft cupid bow's mouth that he so longed to kiss until he could blank out the misery of always feeling on the outside. What did it matter if she knew who he was? It suddenly didn't seem so important to keep that side of his past hidden from her. He took another deep breath and this time let it out in a rush before he could change his mind. 'I'm not Michael Chatsfield's biological son.'

CHAPTER NINE

ISABELLE LOOKED AT him blankly for a moment. 'What?'

He had turned away from her and was in the process of slipping on a bathrobe and waited until he tied the waist ties before he answered. 'My mother had an affair as a payback to my...to Michael early in their marriage. I was the product of that affair.'

She could barely take it in. It was such a shock to her. But how much more of a shock must it have been to him? When had he found out? Why hadn't he mentioned it before now? He was so much of a Chatsfield to her. She couldn't envisage him as anything else. He even looked like his brothers...sort of. They were all tall with dark brown hair, although Ben's was more of a chestnut brown. Their eyes were slightly different but even she and her sisters had different coloured eyes. It didn't make them any less related. 'When did you find out?'

'When I was twenty-nine.'

'*Twenty-nine?*' Isabelle gasped. 'How did you find out? Who told you?'

He rubbed a hand over his face, the action pulling at his features until they were distorted, making him look older than his thirty-four years. 'No one told me.

I might still not have known if I hadn't overheard my parents arguing about it. I confronted them and the truth came out, but only partially. Only my brother Ben knows. James is still in the dark.'

She felt a crushing weight against her chest for how he must have felt. For how he must still be feeling. 'That's terrible…I mean, it must've been such a horrible shock.'

He gave her a wry look. 'And then some.'

She bit down on her lip. 'Could there have been a mistake? Your mother might've been sleeping with both men if it was early in her marriage. Was a paternity test ever done to be absolutely sure?'

'My mother knew from the start. Something about the dates lining up or something. I did my own test to confirm it.'

'Who's your real father?'

His expression became shuttered, as if he was already regretting telling her so much. 'No one important.'

'He doesn't have to be important, Spencer. He's your father. You share his DNA. That's important enough, surely?'

He gave her a black look. 'Thanks for reminding me.'

Isabelle swallowed as a host of possibilities of his parentage flooded her brain. 'He isn't a nice person, then?'

He moved to the windows of the suite, standing with his back to her as he looked out at the view. It was at least thirty seconds, maybe even more, before he spoke. 'He drank. He gambled. He beat up his last partner until she was hospitalised. He's dead now after a drunk-driving accident and I can't say I'm unhappy about it.'

She looked at him standing there, every muscle in his back and shoulders taut with tension. He looked so…so alone. As if there was an invisible wall around him no one could get through. It explained so much about his determination. His ruthless drive to succeed. But why let her in on the secret? 'Why did you tell me?'

He turned to look at her but his expression was still unfathomable. 'You caught me in a weak moment.'

'You don't have weak moments, Spencer.'

He cracked a half-smile. 'Yes, well, where you're concerned it seems I do.'

She moved across to where he was standing, stopping just in front of him so she could touch him on the arm as her gaze meshed with his. 'Thank you.'

'For?'

'For trusting me.'

He raised a cynical brow over one of his eyes. 'Can I trust you? How do I know you won't spill all to the press as a payback?'

Isabelle frowned as her hand fell away from his arm. 'Do you really think I'd do something like that?'

He shrugged. 'I don't know. I guess it's a risk I'm going to have to take.'

'I wouldn't just be hurting you, though, would I?' she said. 'Your mother, Michael and your brothers, one of whom is married to my sister.'

He studied her for a long moment. 'You know the thing that gets me even after all this time?' He didn't wait for her to respond but continued in a hollow-sounding tone. 'I always struggled with feeling wanted in my family. Nothing I could do would ever please my mother or my father. I was a good student. I did well at school and university. But no amount of effort on my part would ever get their attention. It was like they were pretending I wasn't there.'

'That must've been awful for you,' Isabelle said. 'Truly horrible.'

He gave her a vacant smile. 'Yes, well, it could've been worse. I could've been sent to live with my biological father and who knows how I would've turned out?'

Isabelle touched him on the arm again. 'I'm sure you would be just the same as you are now.'

He put his hand over hers and gave it a gentle squeeze, his dark blue eyes searching hers. 'Why are you being so sweet about this?'

She looked at his hand covering hers, the darkness of his on the lightness of hers. They were different and yet alike in more ways than she had been prepared to admit. Driven. Ambitious. Disciplined. Determined. Angry and bitter about how life had dealt them a bad hand. 'Maybe I'm getting tired of being angry all the time.'

He tucked a strand of her hair behind her ear, making her shiver all over at the tender touch. 'I'm not proud of how I handled things when we met. The only thing I can say in my defence is I was young and brash and overly confident. I wanted you and wouldn't stop until I had you.'

Isabelle found it hard to summon up her angst towards him in this atmosphere of newfound intimacy. The fact he'd shared such an important and potentially damaging secret with her suggested a level of trust unlike any she had experienced with anyone else. It made it so much harder to access her anger and bitterness over the takeover.

But maybe that was why the takeover was so important to him. It was his way of proving himself to his family. To pull off the deal of a lifetime, overcoming every obstacle in the way—including her—to take the hotel chain to the top of boutique luxury accommodation. 'Is that why you went after my hotel the way you did? Because you wanted to prove yourself to your family?'

'It's part of it.' He gave a rueful grimace. 'Okay, it's most of it. But I wanted to prove it to myself more than anyone.'

She couldn't stop a little resentment creeping into her tone. 'Couldn't you have picked another hotel?'

He trailed a finger down the curve of her cheek. 'I've always loved The Harrington. What it stands for. The old-world class and sophistication that sets it apart.'

Was he talking about the hotel or her? The look in his eyes and the tone of his voice made her hopes lift. But she just as quickly squashed them. She had no business getting emotionally involved with him. That part of her heart was locked. Bolted. She frowned again, harder, so hard she felt it tug at her forehead. 'But you want to change it. You said I wasn't making the most of its assets.'

'I only want to maximise what you're already doing,' he said. 'Raising the bar above your nearest competitor which is why we need to follow through on our secret shopper mission.'

'How are we going to keep our identities a secret? As soon as we check in they're going to know who we are.'

'I have it sorted.'

She looked at him narrowly. 'How?'

He gave her a twinkling smile. 'Someone has generously given us an accommodation voucher all expenses paid. We just have to turn up.'

'But won't reception want a credit card swipe for incidentals such as the minibar or room service? It's standard practice.'

He lifted a shoulder in a nonchalant shrug. 'The staff on the front desk aren't going to take any notice of what name's on my credit card.'

She gave him a wry look. 'They will when they see it's a black one. Only half a per cent of the population have one of those.'

Something flickered across his darkly handsome features. 'I don't brandish my wealth around like I used to.'

Isabelle frowned at his tone. 'Because you don't feel it's *your* wealth anymore?'

His gaze moved away from hers. 'I'd better let you get to work. We both have a busy day ahead.'

She let out a sigh and picked up her purse from where she had left it on the table next to the sofa. She glanced at him again but he was back at the windows looking out at the view of Central Park. The urge to go to him was strong, almost too strong to resist. But she sensed he needed time and space to gather himself. 'I'll be free tonight if you're still interested.'

He didn't turn around but she noticed his shoulders lost some of their tension. 'I'll look forward to it.'

So will I, she thought. *Much more than I should.*

Much more than is wise.

* * *

Isabelle put the final touches on the meal the kitchen had sent up. The candles were lit, the wine chilled, the lights turned to a muted glow. She had never brought someone back to her suite, or at least not a date. Even her girlfriends—the few she managed to keep in touch with when work allowed—met her in cafés or restaurants. Inviting friends back to her hotel suite had always felt rather odd. It was odd living in a hotel but she had never thought of living anywhere else. Living on-site meant she could sort out problems without delay.

But Spencer's comment about living outside the hotel had struck a distant chord in her. She wondered what it would be like…an apartment of her own, or a town house with a little garden, or a cottage in the Hamptons for when she needed to get out of the frenzied busyness of New York.

The doorbell rang and she smoothed her hands down her hips. Nerves fluttered in her stomach. Her heart skipped a beat. Her insides quivered at the memory of the passion she and Spencer had shared early that morning. Her body had felt jazzy all day from the experience of making love with him.

Having sex, she corrected.

Isabelle opened the door to find him standing there with something dangling from his fingers. 'What on earth is that?' she said.

'A present for Atticus,' he said, handing a toy mouse to her.

She gave him a narrowed look. 'You're bending the rules.'

He smiled and stepped over the threshold. 'I figured

since he can't catch any real ones he might as well have a go at chasing a fake one.'

She closed the door and led the way through to the sitting room area where Atticus was curled up on the one of the sofas. 'I thought you said I had to get rid of him.'

Spencer gave the cat a scratch behind the ears. Atticus slitted his eyes in pleasure and started purring like an engine. 'I feel sorry for him stuck living in a hotel. What sort of place is this for a cat? He should have a garden so he can bask in the sunshine. Don't cats like to do that?'

Isabelle had a feeling he wasn't just talking about the cat. 'Would you like a drink?'

'In a minute,' he said. 'I want to see if Atticus likes his present.'

She watched as he wound up the toy and set it on the floor. Atticus crouched low, tail twitching, and then as soon as Spencer released the toy Atticus sprang off the sofa in pursuit, batting it with his paws while it whirled about crazily, finally subduing it as the wind-up mechanism ran out of puff.

'See?' Spencer smiled up at Isabelle. 'A natural born killer.'

She gave him a hardened look. 'Which is why he's better off locked inside so he can't destroy the wildlife.'

He straightened and took the glass of champagne she had poured. 'How was your day?'

'Fine. Yours?'

He searched her gaze for a moment. 'Any regrets?'

'About what?'

'About this morning.'

Isabelle kept her expression as unreadable as possible. Difficult considering her body was already re-acting to his proximity. 'No.'

He stroked a lazy finger down the underside of her jaw. 'Nor me.' He waited a beat before adding, 'It felt good. Telling you, I mean.'

She gave up trying to control her expression. 'I'm glad you told me but I'm still trying to figure out why me of all people.'

His fingertip gently outlined her mouth, making every nerve fizz and buzz with delight. 'Aren't lovers supposed to share secrets with each other?'

Should she tell him her secret? Isabelle wondered. The painful secret of her loss, the guilt she still felt, the turmoil of emotion she went through every time she heard the word *mother* or saw a mother and child… the overwhelming jealousy she felt…

She wasn't ready to tell him. It was too soon. She didn't know if she could trust him.

She slipped her gaze out of reach of his, concentrating on his mouth instead. 'We don't have that sort of relationship.'

He brought up her chin. 'We could have.'

Isabelle almost lost herself in the dark blue sea of his gaze, only pulling herself back in time as reality dawned. He was charming her. Trying to get her to relax the rules. He wasn't serious about a future with her. He wanted to win this. It was a game to him. She dislodged his hand from her face. 'Ha, ha, like that could ever work,' she said. 'You live in England. I live here.'

'You could move.'

Isabelle rounded on him. 'What, and leave everything I've sacrificed and worked for here? Not going to happen, no matter how good in bed you are.'

His expression tightened like a fist. 'I don't believe you're happy with the life you live. For God's sake, you live in a hotel room with a cat. You haven't had a serious relationship since I don't know when. How can you say you're happy?'

'I didn't say I was happy,' she threw back. 'But who is? You certainly aren't with all your one-night stands and shallow flings, so who are you to say my life sucks?'

He let out a long breath as he pushed his hand through his hair. 'You're right. I'm sorry. I have no right to pass judgement.'

Isabelle bit down on her lip and turned away. 'I'll get dinner sorted.'

'Wait.' His hand came down on her shoulder and turned her to face him. His eyes searched hers for an endless moment. 'I want us to be friends as well as lovers. We don't have to snip and snarl at each other because of what's happened before. Can't we start over?'

Start over?

How easy would life be if she could do that? Just rewind the clock. Press replay. Eradicate all the hurt and pain as if it had never happened.

As if their baby had never happened...

Isabelle moistened her lower lip where her teeth had pressed so firmly. 'You can't wipe away the past. Life doesn't work like that or at least not for me it doesn't.'

He gripped the tops of her shoulders in a firm but gentle hold. 'I know it's difficult to let go. I'm sorry about how I behaved back then. I was too proud and stubborn to fight for what we had. But last night when you stayed with me…that meant something to me, you know? I guess that's why I told you about my father. I saw something in you I knew I could trust.'

Isabelle saw the glint of earnestness in his gaze. Could he be telling the truth? Did he want more than a fling? It was so tempting to relax her armour. But what if she got her hopes crushed all over again? She'd been a sucker for falling for him once. She would be certifiable for doing it twice. 'I think we should stick to the rules for now,' she said. 'I'm not ready for anything else.'

He gave her shoulders a little squeeze, his expression rueful. 'I don't think I've ever wanted to kiss someone more than you right now.'

'I'm not stopping you.'

He gave a lopsided smile. 'You still think you can win this, don't you?'

Isabelle held her breath as his head came closer, his warm minty breath mingling intimately with hers. 'Go on,' she said. 'I dare you.'

His mouth came within a whisker of hers, his lips playing with the corner of her mouth where every sensitive nerve quivered in delight. He moved his lips to the other side of her mouth, and then to her chin, his light stubble grazing her skin, making her knees almost fold beneath her. 'You're the most bewitching woman I've ever met.'

'Save those lines for someone who'll fall for them.'

He pulled back to look at her with a frown. 'You don't think I mean it?'

Isabelle wanted him to mean it. She *ached* for him to mean it. But he'd said similar things before and look how that had turned out. 'I think you're good at getting what you want by any means you can. Flattery, seduction, bending the rules to suit your ends.'

He brushed his thumb over her lower lip. It was something he had done a lot in the past, as if he found her mouth fascinating to touch. She found it thrilling to have him touch it. It made her want him all the more. The need pulsed through her. The need to feel his mouth press hard down on hers, drawing from her a response that came up from her toes and consumed her entire body. 'You don't like me very much, do you?' he said.

'Lust has nothing to do with liking someone.'

His eyes smouldered as they held hers. 'Do you still hate me?'

Isabelle lowered her gaze to his mouth. 'A little.'

A light of triumph sparked in his gaze. 'But not as much as before.'

She pursed her lips. 'I'm sure your ego will survive the fact I'm not going to fall in love with you.'

'Did you ten years ago?'

The question momentarily threw her. She stood looking at him numbly, not wanting to think of how she had felt back then. The hurt, the sense of betrayal and the disappointment of having everything she longed for taken away. No way would she admit how deeply she had fallen for him. It was humiliating enough he had such sensual influence over her even now. But as long as she kept things focused on the physical chemistry they shared she would be safe in a way she hadn't been before. 'I was infatuated with you. It was my first love affair. I was soon over it once I came back to earth.'

Nothing showed on his expression but she got the feeling he was disappointed in her answer. He touched her lower lip again, his eyes hooded. 'Do we have to have dinner straightaway?' he said.

'No, it can wait a bit.'

'Good.' His head came down again as his lips travelled in a blistering trail to the shallow dish between the juncture of her collarbones. 'Because I have other things on my mind right now.'

Isabelle shuddered as his tongue laved her skin, making her senses reel like a spinning top. His body moved closer, so close she could feel the heat and potency of his erection. She pressed against him, all that was feminine in her reaching for all that was male in him. She could feel her inner core contracting in anticipation, the flexing and coiling of intimate muscles. No one could make her more aroused than him. It was like an uncontrollable force moving within her body. It consumed her in a feverish heat that made her blood sizzle inside the network of her veins.

His hands moved from her shoulders to slide down to her hips, pulling her closer until she felt every hard contour of his body. She stroked her hand over him, teasing him with her touch, relishing in the way he surged against her.

'I want you naked,' he said against her neck, his teeth tugging at her skin in a bite that had a hint of danger to it.

Isabelle brought her mouth to within a breath of his, playing with the edges where his stubble grew in spiky bursts. 'So undress me.'

He tugged her silk blouse out of the waist of her pencil slim skirt, and then began to unbutton it, pausing between each release of button from its hole to press a hot kiss to her exposed flesh. By the time he got to the buttons between her breasts she was breathless with excitement. He sucked on each nipple through her bra, teasing her with the expectation of removing the lace barrier so he could take her in his mouth.

He undid the last of the buttons and helped her wriggle out of the blouse until it slipped to the floor in a silken pool. He unhooked her bra and cupped her in his hands, his thumbs moving over her nipples until they were pebble hard and aching for his lips and tongue. He lowered his mouth to each of her breasts in turn, lingering over them, torturing them with the flick and glide of his tongue and the gentle scrape of his teeth.

She was fast losing track of everything but what was happening in her body. The desire she felt for him was surging through her like a bullet train. She couldn't control her response to him even if she wanted to. She was going on primal instinct; she wanted him as badly as he wanted her. She moaned her need, unashamed of the lust that burned and raged in her body.

He pulled down the zipper at the back of her skirt, letting his warm hands glide over her bottom, over her panties first and then below them. The electric shock of his touch on her naked flesh made her shiver in pleasure. She undid his trousers and freed him from his underwear in a frantic mission to subject him to the same heart-stopping torture. He was fully engorged, primed for his possession of her.

She massaged him with her cupped hand, in up and down strokes that made him groan with delight. But he only let her do it for a moment or two before he pulled her hand away. He didn't speak. She wondered if like her he was incapable of it. The needs that raced through her were robbing her of the ability to think, let alone anything else.

He pushed her to the floor, not roughly but with an urgency that spoke of the firestorm of passion that powered through him. He somehow sourced a condom from his nearby trouser pocket, tearing the packet with his teeth and applying it with a deftness that reminded her of his level of experience in comparison to the paucity of hers.

He stroked between her folds, finding her swollen clitoris with devastating accuracy. Her back lifted off the floor as she felt the first tingles of an approaching orgasm. He entered her then with a smooth, thick thrust that triggered her release like a pin being pulled on a grenade. It was just as explosive. Her body clenched him as she shook and shuddered with spasms of rapture, his deepening thrusts escalating her pleasure to previously unknown bounds. She thrashed and bucked and writhed beneath his pumping body, her gasping cries shattering the silence. She clung to him as he finally gave in and spilled. She felt each deep shudder go through him, felt the fine gravel of goose bumps spring up over his back and shoulders where she held him. His breathing was as hectic as hers, his chest rising and falling against her breasts.

'I hope I haven't given you carpet burn,' he said after a long moment.

Isabelle danced her fingertips up and down his spine like she was playing the piano. 'I'll have you know that at The Harrington we only have the very finest in woollen carpets that do *not* give our clientele carpet burn.'

He propped himself up on his elbows to grin at her.

'Maybe I should do a quality control test.' He suddenly rolled, taking her with him so she was straddling him.

Isabelle's loosened hair fell about her breasts, tickling them in the same way his touch had done earlier. The way he was looking at her, his eyes dark with desire, made her feel more powerfully, vibrantly, sensually alive than at any other time of her life. It gave her a sense of boldness she hadn't possessed in the past. She was on top. A position she hadn't adopted before.

She gathered her hair in one hand and pushed it over her left shoulder as she wriggled down so her mouth was within reach of his stirring erection. She sent her tongue the entire length of him, slowly, tantalising him with a delicate caress that made him smother an expletive.

She moved her mouth to just above his groin, in the sensitive region between his belly button and the base of his penis. Licking and stroking with the tip of her tongue, taking little nips as she got closer and closer to her prize, only to back away again, spinning out the anticipation until he was twitching with need.

'You're killing me,' he said in a raw, breathless tone.

She glanced up at him through half-mast lashes. 'I'm not finished with you yet.'

He made a vain attempt to reach for a condom but she batted away his hand and went down to take him fully into her mouth, drawing deeply, sucking and pulling until he let out a long deep groan and then tensed. She lifted her mouth and took over with her hands so she could watch him come. There was something so wickedly exciting about witnessing the spurting flow of his essence, the way it spilled in a creamy fountain over her hand.

'I've always wanted to do that,' she said, handing him a tissue.

He dealt with the practicalities before meeting her gaze with a twinkle in his own. 'You're right. Your carpets are top standard.'

Isabelle leaned forward to press a kiss to his sternum. 'Are you hungry yet?'

'Did you cook for me?'

She sat back. 'No. I don't have a kitchen.'

'So you only eat hotel food?'

'Not always.' She got off him and reached for her bra and panties. 'I go out occasionally.'

He rolled onto his side to watch her dress. 'Don't you get tired of the same menu week after week?'

Isabelle zipped up her dress. 'I make sure the menu is changed regularly.'

He got off the floor and stepped into his trousers, his gaze still trained on her as he zipped them up. 'Can you cook?'

She gave him a quelling look. 'What is this? An interview for a wife? If you want someone to cook for you, then go sleep with a chef. I have better things to do with my time.'

He shrugged on his shirt, still watching her as he did up the buttons. 'Why are you being so defensive?'

'I'm not being defensive. I just think it's a little archaic of you to assume just because I'm a woman that I want to spend my time slaving over a hot oven.'

'You used to love cooking,' he said. 'You told me when we were dating.'

'Yes, well, that was then, this is now.'

'What changed?'

I changed. Isabelle turned for the dining area where

she had set out their meal. 'I have a career that's incredibly important to me. I'm sure you don't spend your spare time whipping up gourmet meals for your lovers.'

He let out a long, frustrated-sounding sigh. 'Why do we always end up arguing?'

She turned to look at him, her shoulders going down at the rueful look on his face. 'I'm not sure…maybe because we both want to prove something.'

'You don't have to prove anything to me.'

Don't I?

Isabelle made herself busy setting the microwave to reheat the food. After a moment she felt him come up behind her. His hands went to her waist, his mouth to the side of her neck. She forgot about the food as she turned in his arms, looking into his blue eyes and seeing the raw need she felt reflected there. 'I don't want to argue with you,' she said. 'It's just I can't bear to lose what I've worked so hard for.'

'We can have what we both want,' he said. 'Can't you see that?'

What did she want?

She was hardly sure of it herself. It was a tangled mix inside her head. She wanted her hotel to remain under her control but he had major share and there was only a slim chance of her winning it back. She wanted him but she didn't want the threat of heartbreak. She wanted intimacy but she didn't want to lose herself in a relationship that might not last beyond a week or two. She yearned for a family to call her own but how could she have it without opening herself up to loss like she had experienced before?

'What do *you* want?' she asked.

'You.'

'For how long?'

His hands tightened on her waist. 'I've never considered anything long term. It's never crossed my radar before but what we have...the feeling I have with you is unlike anything I've had with anyone else. We're good together, Isabelle. Better than good.'

How much of his want of her was tied up in his want of her hotel? The chance to prove himself to his family was his primary motive. She would be foolish and naive to forget that. Her own motivations were just as confusing. She wanted to maintain her family's hold on The Harrington. She had put everything on the line to do that: her life, her happiness, all of her innermost desires, had been sacrificed on the altar of the success of the hotel. 'I can only give you this,' she said. 'A fling is all I want.'

His hands loosened on her waist and then fell away. 'Fine.'

Isabelle let out a breath. 'You're angry.'

'What makes you think that?'

'You're frowning.'

He relaxed his expression. 'I'm not.'

She handed him the salad bowl. 'Why don't you take this through? I'll bring in the chicken once it's heated.'

Spencer carried the bowl with the Greek salad out to the table in the dining area where Isabelle had set up a candlelit setting. It had all the hallmarks of romance and yet he couldn't help feeling it was a sham. She had made her intentions clear. They were ironically the same as his intentions had been ten years ago. She wanted a no-strings fling.

But he felt differently now.

He couldn't put his finger on when or why he had changed. Perhaps it was being with her, seeing her again, touching her again and making love with her. It awakened the feelings he had been trying to ignore. Feelings that niggled at him, reminding him the life he had been living was shallow, pointless, as pointless and shallow as the affairs he had with women he couldn't remember once they left his bed.

How had his life come to that?

Isabelle staying to watch over him last night while he'd been ill had moved him deeply. No one had ever been that close to him before. It had given him a vision of what a relationship—a proper, committed relationship—could be like. One where both parties watched out for each other, allowing each other to grow and reach their potential rather than holding back and limiting or obstructing each other as his parents had done. He wanted more for his life than that. How had it taken him this long to realise it? Wasn't that why he had told her about his biological origins? He had sensed she wouldn't judge him for it. That it would help her connect with him better, to understand what drove him so relentlessly.

He put the salad on the table and wandered over to the bookcase where all the books Isabelle had read were lined up neatly like soldiers in a row. Except for one. It was out of alignment as if it had been shoved in quickly. He went to straighten it but something made him take it off the shelf. It was an anthology of English poetry. He leafed through the pages, recognising so many poems he had studied as a schoolboy: Keats, Coleridge and Wordsworth and Donne—all of the names as familiar to him as old friends.

But then something between the pages fluttered to

the floor. He bent down to pick it up just as he heard Isabelle come in. Her heard her indrawn breath before he registered what he was looking at. His heart gave a painful kick against his breastbone. His stomach hollowed. His mouth went completely dry.

It was an ultrasound image of a tiny foetus.

He swung his gaze to Isabelle's, his heart giving another sickening lurch when he saw the shocked expression on her face. 'What's this?' he said.

She took the photo from him and held it close to her chest. 'I was going to tell you...'

His heart kicked again. 'Tell me what?'

She sank her teeth into her bottom lip as her gaze fell away from his. 'I...I was pregnant.'

Every organ in his body shifted from its foundations as if rocked by an earthquake. He couldn't get his brain to compute the words she'd just said. *Pregnant? She'd been pregnant? Who was the father? Where was the baby?*

He looked at the image again. Swallowed tightly. Painfully.

Isabelle had carried another man's child.

The thought was so foreign, so shocking, to him he couldn't get his mind to accept it.

'When?' His voice came out like a hollow croak.

He saw her throat rise and fall. Saw her teeth pull at her lip and the colour wash into her cheeks. 'Ten years ago.'

Spencer's stomach dropped like an elevator. *'What?'*

Her bottom lip quivered. 'I lost the baby just before the four-month mark.'

He opened and closed his mouth. He couldn't locate his voice. His heart was pounding as if he'd run a marathon without training. He swallowed to clear the blockage in his throat. 'You were pregnant…with *my* child? Why didn't you…?'

'I didn't find out until I got back home.'

'For God's sake, why didn't you tell me then?'

She looked away, still clutching the photo to her chest. 'I was in denial at first. I couldn't believe the test results. It was like a bad dream. I didn't want to be pregnant. Not to you.'

'Thanks.'

She flicked him a glance. 'Not to anyone. I felt too young. I was still missing my own mother. How could I be ready to be a mother myself?'

He couldn't get his mind around the fact he'd got her pregnant. He had planted a child inside her womb. They had made a baby together. It wasn't just a bunch of his cells and hers but a baby. *Their baby.* 'But we used protection.'

'It must've failed.'

Flick knives of guilt slashed through him. Had he been careless? There were times when he'd taken a while to withdraw. What if a condom had leaked or broken? And then there was the way he'd allowed things to end with her. He had dismissed her as if she'd meant nothing to him. She had been carrying his child, his own flesh and blood. He of all people knew how important it was to claim and take responsibility for one's child. He had been robbed of the chance but it was his own fault. 'I don't know what to say…I don't know how to make this right.'

'You can't.'

He came over to where she was standing clutching the photo. 'Can I see it?'

She handed the photo to him. '*Her.* She was not an it.'

He felt something claw-like grab him deep inside his chest. He had fathered a little daughter. A daughter he would never get to meet. She had existed for such a short time. He looked at the image of his little girl. She was tiny, more like a peanut than a baby, but even so he could make out the beginnings of her human form. He had never allowed himself to imagine becoming a father, not since he found out about his origins. The loss of something he hadn't even known he wanted hit him like a blow to the solar plexus.

He'd fathered a little girl.

Emotion thickened his throat until he couldn't swallow or speak. His eyes burned and blurred and he blinked to clear them. 'Did you name her?' he finally managed to ask.

'I called her Olive.'

'Olive.' He tested the name on his tongue. 'That's nice.' He looked at the image again. 'Can I have a copy?'

Isabelle took the photo from him. 'I'll get one made tomorrow.'

Spencer looked at her. 'Who else knows about her?'

She chewed at her lip again. 'Only Sophie.'

He frowned. 'You told no one else? Not even your father and sisters?'

She shook her head.

'Why didn't you tell me?' he asked.

'I told you why.'

'Damn it, Isabelle, I had a right to know. You should've contacted me immediately.'

Her eyes flashed at him. 'So you could do what? Talk me into having an abortion?'

Spencer's throat was raw as he swallowed. 'You think I would've pressured you to do that? Do you really?'

She flung herself away from him, tucking the photo back inside her book and putting it back in amongst the others. 'I didn't know what to think.' Her hand fell away from the bookshelf as she turned to look at him again. 'I thought you'd betrayed me with that bet. I thought the very last thing you'd want from me after that was a request for child support.'

A toxic turmoil of emotions was churning his gut, a mix of guilt and shame and regret. 'I still think you should've told me. Either way I could've helped you.'

She gave him a cutting look through glittering eyes. 'Come on, Spencer. Be honest with yourself. You would've freaked out if I'd told you I was pregnant. You would never have stood by me.'

'How do you know?' He had to force himself to keep his voice down. 'How can you possibly know how I would've reacted when you didn't give me a chance *to* react?'

She stood in front of the bookcase with her back turned resolutely towards him, her arms wrapped tightly around her slim body. Everything about her posture locked him out. It made another wave of righteous anger ricochet through him. How could she freeze him out over something so life changing? How could she have kept this secret from him for so long?

But then he realised her shoulders were shaking. His chest seized. Emotions he hadn't realised he was capable of feeling clogged his throat. *He had done this.* He had all but ruined her life. His selfish pursuit of her had left her devastated and terrifyingly alone. She hadn't told anyone but her closest friend about the pregnancy. What right did he have to be angry? He had no idea of what she must have gone through.

He went over to her and gently turned her to face him. Twin tracks of tears were streaming from her eyes and her bottom lip was quivering in spite of the clamp of her teeth. He had never seen her cry. She was always so stoic, so strong and feisty and fighting from her corner with two fists up and ready. He caught a glimpse of the young terrified girl she had been and another fist of guilt grabbed at his guts. 'I'm sorry,' he said, gently blotting the tears away with the pad of his thumb. 'I know that's never going to be enough but I'm truly sorry.'

She swallowed and blinked a couple of times. 'I was so frightened…I didn't know what to do…'

He held her to his chest where his heart was still contracting with painful spasms. 'I don't know what to say. I feel like I've ruined your life.'

She pulled back to look up at him through reddened eyes. The pain in her gaze made his insides clench again. 'I felt so confused about it at first. I was in denial for weeks. I did test after test hoping each one would be negative. But then I got used to the idea… I started to plan. I thought about how it would be to have a baby, someone to need me, someone I could love more than life itself. Like the way my mum had loved my sisters and me. I wanted to have a chance to do that…to be the sort of mum who would give everything up for her children.'

Spencer cradled her head in his hands, stroking her

cheeks with his thumbs. 'I can't bear to think of what you went through.'

Her chin wobbled again. 'I felt so alone when I... when I lost her. Walking out of that hospital the day after was like leaving half of myself behind. I walked past families coming in to visit other women who'd given birth. Dads with little kids in tow, grandparents and uncles and aunties carrying flowers and teddy bears and beautifully wrapped gifts. It was like everyone was deliberately torturing me for failing at being a mother.'

He pulled her back against his chest, holding her as his own eyes burned. 'You didn't fail, darling girl. You were a perfect mother to her. You loved her and wanted her and did all you could to protect her.'

She let out a shuddering sigh against his chest. 'I wish I'd told you. You're right, you had a right to know.'

He gently stroked her hair, his emotions in a twisted knot that seemed to be trapped halfway down his throat like a handful of chopped razor blades. 'This isn't about me. It's about you. What you went through. I can't rewind the clock. I can't undo what's happened no matter how much I want to.'

She eased out of his hold with a fragile-looking smile. 'I'm sorry about dinner but I don't feel hungry anymore. I'm exhausted. I think I might go to bed.'

He couldn't hear an invitation to join her, which either meant she was withdrawing from him or needed time alone. Or both. But then, didn't he feel exactly the same? He tucked another strand of hair behind her ear. 'Do you want to be alone?'

She didn't meet his gaze but addressed his shirt buttons. 'Would you mind?'

Disappointment sliced through him but he decided against trying to change her mind. His world had tipped on its axis, like hers had done ten years ago. He needed time to process it. To understand how he was going to manage things from here. He brushed his thumb over her lower lip. 'Let's have breakfast tomorrow. I'll bring it.'

She gave another ghost of a smile but it didn't get anywhere close to involving her eyes. 'That'd be nice.'

Isabelle closed the door and leant back against it after she'd seen him out. For a moment there she thought he was going to insist on staying. She could see the moment of indecision in his gaze as it held hers. She even thought he was going to kiss her. But he must have remembered the forfeit. If he broke the rules he would pay.

A nut of anger reformed in her belly. Of course he wouldn't break the rules. He still wanted to win this, no matter what emotional hits she threw at him. What could be more of an emotional knockout than knowing you'd fathered a child ten years ago?

Yes, but you pushed him away, a tiny voice reminded her.

Isabelle dismissed it. Of course she'd pushed him away. But if he cared wouldn't he have pushed back? Insisted on staying to comfort her even if it meant he lost his stupid shares?

No, it would be business as usual with him come tomorrow. She could predict what he would do. He would have a plan in place once he'd had time to think things through.

But this time she would be better prepared.

CHAPTER TEN

SPENCER SPENT A wretched night watching the clock go round as he wrestled with every demon that possessed him: the commitment fears that plagued him, the claustrophobic sense of his life being controlled by others, of not being worthy, of not having all the facts on the table. Of not being in control.

He thought about the baby. What would little Olive be like if she'd survived? Would she have looked like Isabelle or him or a combination of both? What sort of father would he have made? Would he have been ready for fatherhood in the way Isabelle had been ready for motherhood?

The doubts fluttered like moths at the edges of his conscience. What *would* he have done if she had told him straight up? That was the thought that plagued him the most. Unsettled him to the point where he shied away from thinking about it like a horse does at a difficult jump. He could actually feel the physicality of it—a jerking, pulling-away sensation in his stomach every time he tried to picture the scenario of Isabelle facing him with the news of her pregnancy.

Spencer stood outside her suite the next morning with a breakfast hamper he'd sourced from catering.

Why was it taking her so long to answer the door? He knocked again, straining his ears for the sound of her footsteps. Had last night upset her so much she wasn't able to face him this morning? Should he have stayed to comfort her? God, why hadn't he stayed?

Because you would have lost the two per cent.

It was confronting to face his competitive streak head-on. He didn't want to be the type of person who would put business before someone he cared about. But he had worked *so* hard for this takeover. Years and years of putting in long hours, living a life out of a suitcase instead of settling in one place because he had something to prove. Not just to his family, but also to himself. Maybe only to himself.

The door opened and Isabelle's cool expression felt like a gust of cold air over his heart. 'I've changed my mind about breakfast,' she said.

'Can we talk?'

She pressed her lips together for a moment. 'If you insist.'

'I do.'

She stepped back from the door with a 'whatever' shrug of one slim silk-clad shoulder.

Spencer put the hamper on the nearest surface before he came to stand in front of her. He searched her features but she was keeping her emotions under tight control, although there was an unnerving hardness to her whisky-brown gaze as it met his. 'How did you sleep?' he asked to break the ringing silence.

'Fine. You?'

He scraped a hand through his still-damp hair. 'Terribly.'

She didn't respond other than to stand with her arms folded, her gaze still centred on his.

He let out a long breath. 'I can't undo what's happened, Isabelle. No one can. But I can try and make it up to you now.'

'How?'

It was only one word and yet it felt like a sucker punch to his guts. *How indeed?* 'We can start again,' he said. 'We're good together. Better than good. I should've realised that ten years ago. But maybe I did and that's why I pulled away...if that makes sense.'

Her chin came up to a combative height. 'Would you have offered to marry me if I'd told you about the baby?'

'If that's what you'd wanted.'

She gave a harsh-sounding laugh. 'And how long do you think that would've lasted? We're totally unsuitable.'

'I disagree.'

She rolled her eyes and turned away. 'You were twenty-four years old. You would never have settled down to the responsibility of marriage. You're not ready even now. The most you'll commit to is a week or two fling.'

Spencer stepped up behind her and put his hands on her shoulders and turned her to face him. 'We can start again. We can get married and have another baby.'

Her top lip curled and her eyes flashed with fire. 'You insensitive jerk.'

'What's wrong?'

She pulled out of his hold, rubbing at her arms as if his touch had tainted her. 'You don't want to marry me. That's just your guilt proposing.'

'I want us to be together,' he said. 'I don't care if it's through marriage or whatever but I want us to be a couple.'

She threw him a contemptuous glance. 'You want my hotel. Not me.'

Spencer took her by the hands, shocked at how cold and stiff and unyielding they were—like two blocks of ice. 'Listen to me, Isabelle. I want you. Not because of the hotel. I couldn't give a stuff about the hotel. I want you.'

Her chin lifted. 'Prove it.'

He frowned. 'What else can I say to convince you?'

Her eyes challenged his. 'Give me the two per cent.'

His hands tightened on hers before he released her. 'I can't do that. Not that.'

Anything but that.

How could she ask it of him? Or was that the whole point? She wanted to win and was using blackmail to do it. He would have to give up the one thing he had worked so hard for. The one thing he needed to prove to his family he was a success in his own right. The one thing he needed to prove to himself he finally belonged.

He couldn't do it.

Her expression was as cold as marble. 'Then I think it's time you left. Our fling is over. I have nothing more to say to you.'

'Is this really how you want to end this?'

'It's your choice.'

'Damn it, you're asking the impossible.'

She gave him a flinty look. 'What's impossible is you thinking you can control me. I know how your mind works. You thought you could win me over with a few insincere endearments, a few flashy gifts and hot sex. But guess what? You failed. I don't love you. I don't even like you.'

Spencer clenched his jaw so hard he felt his molars grind together. 'I don't believe you.'

She lifted a shoulder in a careless shrug. 'Go on deluding yourself. It's no skin off my nose.'

'We made a baby together, Isabelle. Doesn't that mean anything to you?'

Her eyes pulsed with bitterness. 'Don't you *dare* bring her into this.'

He let out a gusty breath, his emotions so messed up he could barely think. He was angry with Isabelle for locking him out, furious and frustrated, and yet a part of him felt so guilty about what she'd gone through alone he wanted to wrap her in his arms and never let her go.

His feelings for her had always confused him. Love was something he avoided feeling. But to hear her say she didn't even like him made him feel…empty. She had slept with him and yet not given anything of herself other than her body.

Just like you have done for years with every lover.

Spencer backed away from the thought. It was too confronting. Too shaming to acknowledge the shallowness of his life up until now. He needed more time to think. Less than twenty-four hours ago he'd thought all he had to contend with was Isabelle's anger about that stupid bet and the takeover. The new knowledge of his almost-fatherhood was too raw. He needed more time to process the cauldron of emotions that was burning a cavernous hole in his chest. 'I'll talk to you later today, over dinner or something. We both need time to think about where we go from here.'

Her arms were folded across her body in her classic keep-away-from-me pose. 'I've already decided.'

A sinkhole hollowed his insides at her implacable look. But he refused to show her how much her stand-off was hurting him. 'Fine. Have it your way.' He scooped up his jacket where he'd left it on the back of the sofa near Atticus. The cat blinked up at him through slitted eyes as if to say, *You're leaving already?* Spencer stopped to give him a quick pat. 'You deserve much better than this, buddy.'

Isabelle sent him a venomous glare. 'He was perfectly happy until you showed up.'

Spencer arched a brow as his hand wrapped around the doorknob. 'Was he?'

Isabelle stormed into her office five minutes later. 'Cancel all of my appointments,' she said to Laura. 'I'm heading out of town for a few days.'

Laura swivelled on her chair to face her. 'Do you want me to book Atticus into a cattery?'

'No. I'm taking him with me.'

'Where are you going?'

Isabelle wondered if it was wise to tell her secretary in case Spencer tried to milk her for details. But if anything went wrong while she was away it was important for Laura to be able to contact her. 'I'm going to a cottage in the Hamptons. I found it online last night. It's pet friendly.'

'I think it's about time you took a break from things,' Laura said. 'You haven't had a holiday in ages. Is Mr Chatsfield going with you?'

Isabelle glared at her. 'What on earth gives you the impression I would go away with him?'

Laura shifted her lips from side to side. 'Pardon me, but I thought you two were getting along famously.'

Isabelle gave a scoffing laugh. 'As if. I hate him more than I thought it possible to hate anyone.'

'Always a good sign.'

She frowned. 'What's that supposed to mean?'

Laura looked up from her typing. 'It's a two-sided coin. Hate and love. All it takes is a simple flip and there you have it—one or the other.'

Isabelle pressed her lips together. 'Don't call me unless it's an emergency.'

'How long will you be away?'

'A week,' she said. 'I don't trust Spencer to refurbish the place in my absence. I can just imagine what he would do. Probably install a brothel or something.'

Laura sat back in her chair. 'Is running away the right way to handle him?'

Isabelle bristled. 'I'm not running away.'

Laura gave her a speaking look.

She let out a long sigh. 'Okay, so I'm running away, but he confuses me. I don't know how to handle him.'

'Men are like that. They don't come with a user manual, more's the pity.'

Isabelle slammed the drawer on her desk. 'Do you know what he did?'

'Tell me.'

'He asked me to marry him. Can you believe that? The hide of him.' She stomped across the room to snatch her phone charger out of the power outlet. 'I wouldn't marry him if he was the last man on earth.' The power cord refused to budge so she had to give it an almighty tug that nearly pulled out the whole power point. 'Or in the universe.'

Laura's lips twitched. 'No, of course you wouldn't.'

'And I'm not going to his stupid ball,' Isabelle ranted. 'I don't care how much money he raises for charity. I'm not going to have my nose publicly rubbed in the fact he's taken my hotel off me.'

'No, of course you don't.'

Isabelle stopped pacing to look at her secretary. A bubble of emotion came up from deep inside her and she had to swallow to keep it contained. 'The thing is…ten years ago I would've given anything to hear him say those words.'

Isabelle blinked back the stinging tears. 'Do you know what I hate the most about him?'

'Tell me.'

Her bottom lip quivered so much she had to bite down on it before she could speak. 'He's so…so much of what I dreamed of as a young girl as a future husband. Someone who was strong and ambitious and yet caring and gentle when he needed to be.'

'Very good reasons for hating him.' Laura nodded sagely.

Isabelle turned for the door. 'If he asks where I am don't tell him.'

'Under any circumstances?'

Isabelle thought about it for a beat. 'If he wants to give me the two per cent shares back, then yes. Tell him where I am.'

CHAPTER ELEVEN

THREE DAYS LATER Spencer looked out of the window of his office at The Harrington. The weather was dismal which perfectly matched his mood. The hotel was just another hotel without Isabelle's presence. It was still stylish and functioned at a high level but the atmosphere was different.

Like your life.

This time he didn't shy away from the thought. He drew it in close and examined it. Put it under the microscope of his conscience. His life was enviable to a lot of people. He had money, he had friends and family, he had a career he loved, and yet something was missing.

Isabelle.

The one woman who had shown him what he was capable of being: a friend, a lover, a protector, a mentor.

A father.

He was used to the word now. He embraced it. He held it close to his heart. He wanted to tell people about his little daughter. He wanted the world to know he loved her even though he had never met her and would never do so.

Why had he walked out on Isabelle again? Hadn't he learned anything in the past decade? She always pushed him away when she was hurt.

He had hurt her.

He was continuing to hurt her the longer he held majority share of the hotel. The only way he could prove his feelings for her was to give them back. It would cause all sorts of dramas with his family, but right now he didn't care.

If things had been different he and Isabelle could have had their own family by now. His chest squeezed like a clamp was around his heart every time he thought of that ultrasound image of his little baby girl.

How had it taken him so long to realise he loved Isabelle? Wasn't the fact he'd broken all his dating rules with her ten years ago the biggest clue of all? He had seen something in her that spoke to him on a level no one else had ever reached. She understood him—his drive, his ambition and his need for control—because she had the same qualities. She had sacrificed so much for the sake of the hotel and he had swanned in and taken it as if it was a trophy at a competition.

Life wasn't a competition.

It was a delicate balance of meeting other people's needs and having your own needs met. He hadn't had his needs fully met until he met Isabelle. He loved that she was strong enough to stand her ground with him. She fought from her corner with the passion and drive that was an elemental part of her personality.

He loved her far too much to lose her a second time. His family might scoff at his sentimentality but this was one time when he was glad he wasn't truly a Chatsfield.

He was his own man.

And when a man had to do what a man had to do, he simply got on with it.

Isabelle walked down to the jetty late in the afternoon just as she had done for the past three days. The sun was shining but there was a cool breeze coming in off the water. The small island she was staying on had a series of privately owned cottages. Hers was the smallest but it had the nicest view. Atticus loved the suntrap of the little garden out the back. Every morning he sauntered out, stretched his back, gave a wide yawn and then curled into a ball on top of a lemon-scented geranium and slept for the entire day.

She envied him. She hadn't slept a wink the whole time she'd been on the island because all she could think about was how much she wished Spencer were here with her.

Yes, even though she hated him.

At least she felt alive when he was around her. He made her want more out of life than living in a suite in a hotel. He made her want more than a casual date now and again. He made her want to be kissed and bought gorgeous gifts and flowers and called by loving endearments, and he made her want to be held all night long so she felt treasured and protected and safe.

Damn him for making her want those things. Those things she had spent the past decade teaching herself not to want. He had no right to storm back into her life and stir up all those emotions she'd locked away. She couldn't get them back under control. It was like trying to refold a paper map. It was darn near impossible.

The sound of a boat skimming along the water in

the bay brought her head up. Isabelle held her hand up to shade her eyes from the afternoon slant of the sun. It was a flash-looking speedboat with red and white and black stripes along the sides and a powerful outboard engine that gave a throaty roar as it turned for the jetty.

A shiver ran over her body as she watched the tall dark-haired man behind the wheel expertly dock the boat and tie it to the jetty. He jumped from the boat to the jetty and came towards her carrying a huge bunch of flowers that looked a little worse for wear after their trip across the wind-whipped water, what looked like a large box of chocolates and a tiny velvet jeweller's box.

Isabelle swallowed a tight lump in her throat. Was she dreaming? Had she somehow conjured up this exact scenario? She didn't allow herself to get too ahead of herself. She kept her emotions in check, her voice cool and her posture collected. 'I hope you're not going to kiss me, because if you do that's every single rule bro—*mmm...*'

The rest of her sentence was smothered by Spencer's mouth as it came down on hers. She wound her arms around his neck and gave herself up to his kiss, swept away by the desperation of it, the heat and potency and promise of it.

The flowers flopped to the wooden jetty, the chocolates were squashed between their bodies and the jeweller's case was gripped tightly in Spencer's hand as he held Isabelle to him.

He lifted his mouth off hers to look down at her. 'I love you. I don't care if you don't love me back but I just had to tell you. I don't care about the shares. You can have as many as you want. Just say you'll give me a chance to make it up to you for all the hurt I've caused. Give me a chance, darling. Please?'

Isabelle blinked back tears. 'I can't believe you came. I wasn't game enough to hope. I've been so used to being unhappy I expect to be disappointed. It's easier that way, you know?'

He pressed a tender kiss to her mouth, and then to each of her eyelids, her nose, her chin and her mouth again. 'I do know. I think that's why I've been gadding about without settling for the past decade. I've been looking for what we had but I could never find it. I only just realised the other day I could only have it with you.'

Isabelle gazed into his beloved dark blue eyes. 'I'm so sorry I didn't tell you earlier about the baby. You're right. I should have told you as soon as I found out.'

He captured her hand and pressed it to his mouth. 'I can't bear the thought of you going through that alone. I can't help thinking if I'd been around to support you, you might not have had a miscarriage. I can never forgive myself for that.'

'It's not your fault,' Isabelle said. 'It's no one's fault. I've accepted that now. It wasn't our time.'

He brushed the windblown hair back off her face with a tender touch. 'There's another thing I realised. I wanted The Harrington because I thought it would prove something to myself and to my family. But if I'm nothing without it, how can I be something with it? It's just a block of bricks and mortar. It doesn't define me as a person. Only my relationship with the ones I love and who love me back can do that.'

Isabelle smiled in blissful happiness. 'I've been a

victim of that either/or thinking too. Instead of thinking yours or mine why don't we think ours?'

He hugged her so tightly the chocolates didn't stand a chance. They fell out of the squished box and landed on the jetty in a scattered pile at their feet.

'The seagulls are going to think their Christmases have come all at once,' Isabelle said, laughing.

'That reminds me.' Spencer opened his tightly clenched hand to reveal the ring box. 'Will you marry me?'

She opened the box to see a gorgeous solitaire diamond winking at her. It was in a classic setting, elegant and simple and yet unmistakably precious. She couldn't have picked better herself. 'It's beautiful...'

He slipped it over her ring finger and held her hand close to his heart, his eyes meshing with hers. 'Is that a yes?'

Isabelle smiled. 'Yes.'

He hugged her again, holding her tightly as if he never wanted to let her go. 'Let's get married as soon as possible. We could have our reception at the hotel instead of the ball. We can still raise heaps of money for charity. More probably. Who wouldn't pay a packet to see two sworn enemies marry? What do you say?'

She touched his face as if she couldn't quite believe he was really standing there saying all the things she most wanted to hear. 'I couldn't think of anything nicer. But do you think we could have our honeymoon here?'

'Why?'

'Because Atticus loves it here,' she said. 'I've never seen him so happy.'

Spencer grinned. 'Maybe we should buy a little weekender here for him. An urban cat needs to get out of town occasionally, right?'

Isabelle linked her arm through his as they walked up towards the cottage. 'Do you know I've been thinking the very same thing. This place is an absolute gold mine. We could buy up some of the properties and do them up into luxurious boutique accommodation. We could call it The Harrington in the Hamptons. Or The Chatsfield by the Sea? What do you think?'

Spencer smiled at the sparkle of enthusiasm shining in her eyes. Her beautiful face was alive with excitement and energy and hope for the future. A hope he could feel spreading inside his chest where a hollow space used to be. 'I think that's a fabulous idea,' he said.

* * * * *

MILLS & BOON®
Hardback – August 2015

ROMANCE

MILLS & BOON®
Large Print – August 2015

ROMANCE

The Billionaire's Bridal Bargain	Lynne Graham
At the Brazilian's Command	Susan Stephens
Carrying the Greek's Heir	Sharon Kendrick
The Sheikh's Princess Bride	Annie West
His Diamond of Convenience	Maisey Yates
Olivero's Outrageous Proposal	Kate Walker
The Italian's Deal for I Do	Jennifer Hayward
The Millionaire and the Maid	Michelle Douglas
Expecting the Earl's Baby	Jessica Gilmore
Best Man for the Bridesmaid	Jennifer Faye
It Started at a Wedding...	Kate Hardy

HISTORICAL

A Ring from a Marquess	Christine Merrill
Bound by Duty	Diane Gaston
From Wallflower to Countess	Janice Preston
Stolen by the Highlander	Terri Brisbin
Enslaved by the Viking	Harper St. George

MEDICAL

A Date with Her Valentine Doc	Melanie Milburne
It Happened in Paris...	Robin Gianna
The Sheikh Doctor's Bride	Meredith Webber
Temptation in Paradise	Joanna Neil
A Baby to Heal Their Hearts	Kate Hardy
The Surgeon's Baby Secret	Amber McKenzie

MILLS & BOON®
Hardback – September 2015

ROMANCE

MILLS & BOON®
Large Print – September 2015

ROMANCE

The Sheikh's Secret Babies	Lynne Graham
The Sins of Sebastian Rey-Defoe	Kim Lawrence
At Her Boss's Pleasure	Cathy Williams
Captive of Kadar	Trish Morey
The Marakaios Marriage	Kate Hewitt
Craving Her Enemy's Touch	Rachael Thomas
The Greek's Pregnant Bride	Michelle Smart
The Pregnancy Secret	Cara Colter
A Bride for the Runaway Groom	Scarlet Wilson
The Wedding Planner and the CEO	Alison Roberts
Bound by a Baby Bump	Ellie Darkins

HISTORICAL

A Lady for Lord Randall	Sarah Mallory
The Husband Season	Mary Nichols
The Rake to Reveal Her	Julia Justiss
A Dance with Danger	Jeannie Lin
Lucy Lane and the Lieutenant	Helen Dickson

MEDICAL

Baby Twins to Bind Them	Carol Marinelli
The Firefighter to Heal Her Heart	Annie O'Neil
Tortured by Her Touch	Dianne Drake
It Happened in Vegas	Amy Ruttan
The Family She Needs	Sue MacKay
A Father for Poppy	Abigail Gordon

MILLS & BOON®

Why shop at millsandboon.co.uk?

Each year, thousands of romance readers find their perfect read at millsandboon.co.uk. That's because we're passionate about bringing you the very best romantic fiction. Here are some of the advantages of shopping at www.millsandboon.co.uk:

* **Get new books first**—you'll be able to buy your favourite books one month before they hit the shops

* **Get exclusive discounts**—you'll also be able to buy our specially created monthly collections, with up to 50% off the RRP

* **Find your favourite authors**—latest news, interviews and new releases for all your favourite authors and series on our website, plus ideas for what to try next

* **Join in**—once you've bought your favourite books, don't forget to register with us to rate, review and join in the discussions

Visit **www.millsandboon.co.uk**
for all this and more today!